Chicago Public Library
P9-EMP-154
The ghost sitter

DISCARD
MAR 2003

Other books by

Peni R. Griffin

Vikki Vanishes

The Maze

The Brick House Burglars

Switching Well

The Treasure Bird

Hobkin

A Dig in Time

Otto from Otherwhere

the GHOST SITTER

the GHOST SITTER

PENI R. GRIFFIN

Dutton Children's Books / New York

Library of Congress Cataloging-in-Publication Data
Griffin, Peni R.
The ghost sitter / by Peni R. Griffin.— 1st ed.
p. cm.
Summary: When she realizes that her new house is haunted by the ghost of a ten-year-old girl who used to live there, Charlotte tries to help her find peace.
ISBN 0-525-46676-2
[1. Ghosts—Fiction. 2. Brothers and sisters—Fiction.] I. Title.
PZ7.G88136 Gh 2001 [Fic]—dc21 00-065859

Published in the United States by Dutton Children's Books,
a division of Penguin Putnam Books for Young Readers
345 Hudson Street, New York, New York 10014
www.penguinputnam.com

Designed by Amy Berniker
Printed in USA First Edition
10 9 8 7 6 5 4 3 2 1

For everyone who baby-sat us in Panora, Iowa

Contents

the GHOST SITTER

Prologue

Susie dove up, away from the pain, into the hot blue sky. A hawk dodged her lazily. A solid-looking white thunderhead dissolved into cool mist around and through her. She rose until the sky darkened to midnight and stars exploded across her vision like fireworks.

Fireworks.

Gloria.

She should be looking after Gloria while the neighborhood kids set off fireworks in the street.

Susie jackknifed and dove back toward the cloud-wrapped earth below, which looked nothing like the globe at school. If asked to find Texas with her eyes, she could not have done so, but she knew where to go. Air whistled in her ears as she dove, down, down, down, through the thunderhead, startling a buzzard. She picked out her house from all the nearly identical houses on nearly identical cul-de-sacs in the subdivision on the edge of town: the gray-blue shingle roof, the baby peach tree in the backyard, the new Chevy in the driveway, the flag drooping from the flagstaff by the front door.

Firecrackers popped and sparked in the dusk. A boy on the corner lit a serpent's egg and stepped back to watch it uncoil in a shower of fire, holding out his arm in front of his little sister. Protecting her, the way Susie was supposed to protect Gloria.

Susie had last seen Gloria in the driveway, but that was ages ago. A quick search up and down the street assured her that she hadn't wandered off to any of the neighbors. Maybe Mama had brought her in. Susie ducked in through the roof and found herself hovering under the ceiling of Gloria's room.

Blocks and stuffed toys strewed the floor. The window stood open, letting in the burnt-powder and barbecue smell of the Fourth of July. Gloria hunched in the middle of her bed, her rump in the air, her curly brown head surrounded by her chubby arms. The room vibrated with misery. Susie sank down and rubbed her little sister's back. "Glo? Glo, honey, what's wrong?"

Glo hiccuped, flinging herself against Susie's side, hugging her fiercely. "They said you were gone!" she gulped. "They said you wouldn't come back!"

"Who said?" asked Susie, stroking her hair.

"The doctors told Mama you'd never come back. You won't go away, will you? You'll stay right here forever and ever?"

"Of course I will," said Susie.

"Promise?"

"Promise." Susie drew a bold X on her chest. "Cross my heart and hope to die, stick a needle in my eye. I'll stay right here forever. Okay?"

"Okay." Gloria rested, a warm lump against Susie's cool side. "We're not going to the fireworks. And it's my fault. But maybe now that you're back, we can go."

Wanting to wipe her sister's tear-streaked face, Susie pulled at a tissue in the box on the nightstand, but she couldn't get a grip on the paper somehow. "Shh," she said. "It's not your fault. It's mine. I'll go talk to them."

"No! Don't go anywhere! You promised!" Gloria clung to her, and Susie rocked her back and forth. "Sing 'Worms.' "

"You're a weird kid, Glo," said Susie, but she sang:

"Nobody loves me, everybody hates me,
I'm going to the garden to eat worms.

Ulp! goes one! Ulp! goes two!
Ulp! goes number three!
Now everybody loves me, nobody hates me,
Better urp up them worms.
Urp! goes one! Urp! goes two!
Urp! goes number three!"

It was the world's strangest lullaby, but it worked. Gloria's body became heavy and still, her breathing deep and regular. As Susie bent to kiss her, she heard the door open. "Glo?" said Mama.

"Shh." Susie turned her head. "She's asleep. I'm sorry—"

"Poor little thing," said Mama. "She's all worn out."

Susie stopped, her feelings hurt. Mama never interrupted! Then she noticed her mother's red eyes, her puffy nose. Her trim new red, white, and blue sundress, identical to Susie's, was crumpled and dirty, and her fresh perm was disheveled. "Mama, I'm sorry I went away, and I won't do it ever again. I promise. Mama?"

Mama knelt beside the bed and reached through Susie, shuddering, as she folded Gloria's sleeping figure in her arms. "Oh, Glo," she whispered. "What do we do now? It can't be true, it can't be. Susie—" Her voice turned into a long sob.

"Mama, what is it? I didn't mean to leave, honest I didn't. Please say it's okay. Mama? Please?" Susie's arms went straight through her mother's body. The sobbing intensified. Gloria stirred. Mama, shaking, kissed the top of her head.

"Mama?"

Mama left the room, crying in shrill, wailing gulps. Susie fluttered after her. Across the hall and into the living room she went, Susie calling her, trying to get a grip on her arms, her clothes, anything! Daddy, on the couch beneath the picture window, held out his arms, and Mama almost fell into them. Together they sat on the couch, rocking back and forth, crying.

Daddy crying? Daddy *never* cried!

Susie cried, too, trying to wiggle in between them, and succeeding all too well. Every time she touched them, their crying got worse and shuddered through her also. Outside, fireworks snapped and stuttered as children shouted. Inside, the darkness gathered in the corners of the living room, and no one turned on the lights.

"I'm cold," murmured Mom as Susie's arms passed through her. "Who would think you could be cold on the Fourth of July?"

"I wish those kids would go in," whispered Dad. "I hear those fireworks—"

"It's my fault, isn't it? If I'd been paying attention—"

"Shh, shh! Maxine! It's nobody's fault!"

"What's nobody's fault?" demanded Susie. "Why are we crying?"

But they didn't answer.

Susie let go and floated above them. For the first time it occurred to her that there was something wrong with the situation, and with her. "I'm dreaming, right?" she asked. "This is all a bad dream, and I want to wake up now!"

Susie knew one surefire way of waking herself. Shooting up through the roof, she stood on the rain gutter above the backyard. Moxie, their terrier, raised his head, ears pricked, and leaped to his feet, wagging his tail and barking. "Oh, hush," Susie called down. "I can't hurt myself in a dream." Deliberately, she stepped off the roof, fighting the impulse to take control of the fall and fly or dive instead.

Compared to the dive back to earth, the distance from the roof to the ground was nothing. She covered it in a couple of seconds—and kept going, falling through a swiftly tickling layer of Bermuda grass, through a warm, thick layer of soil and into the cool embrace of limestone bedrock.

If she let herself, would she fall straight through to the layer of lava that her science teacher said wrapped the center of the earth?

Susie braked and swam upward, shaking all over. It was harder to swim than to dive. Slower. It left more time to think. What had happened? Gloria and Moxie—playing in the driveway—Moxie, scared of the fireworks—

wriggling when picked up. Susie tried to remember, but between her taking Moxie into the garage and her soaring through the sky, a barrier of pain stood across her mind—pain, overwhelming guilt, and failure. Guilt about what? Failure to do what? Pain of what?

How long had she been underground?

When she broke the surface of the backyard, the sun shone bright and hot. Moxie barked, but she could not see him. Following the sound to the front of the house, she saw a moving van from the same company that had moved them into the new house only a few months ago. The moving men carried furniture out—the new couch, Daddy's favorite armchair, Mama's gleaming new refrigerator. Mama and Daddy loaded the trunk of the Chevy with suitcases. Gloria slumped on the grass beside Moxie's travel cage. Susie ran up. "Glo? What's happening?"

Moxie threw a fit, trying to fight his way out of the travel cage. Glo looked up with wide eyes. "Where've you been?" she demanded. "We're moving."

"Moving? But—Gloria, what's happened?"

"You left," said Gloria. "You promised you wouldn't, and you *did*!"

"Why are we moving?"

"Because you left!"

Mama picked up Gloria. "C'mon, Glo," she said. "It's time to head over to the new house."

"Susie's here," said Gloria, pointing.

Mama took a quick breath, almost like a sob, and shook her head, not even looking. "Susie's gone, Glo."

"But I'm right here!" protested Susie, flinging herself at her mother—and plunging into her, as if into scalding water. Mama shivered, then carried Gloria off, screaming.

Susie ran after them, trying to climb into the backseat of the Chevy, alongside Gloria, but a barrier sprang up, gray and humming like a cloud of gnats, at the car door, and she could not penetrate it. Daddy retrieved Moxie's cage, and the little dog whined as he pushed it through Susie's body into the backseat. She threw her arms around Daddy's neck, but that didn't even slow him down.

Susie tried to run after the car but bounced back as she reached the street. Desperately she fought the humming barrier, but it was like fighting Jell-O.

In the back window of the Chevy, framed by the tail fins, Gloria's face appeared small and white. Her arm waved like a flag of surrender. Unable to do anything else, Susie waved back.

1

The Blue House

Moving was a heck of a way to spend the first day of vacation, but Charlotte was too glad to get out of the apartment to mind much. Besides, Mom, Bart, and the movers were doing all the hard work. Her only job, oh joy, was to keep Brandon out from underfoot. Bart set up the playpen under the big peach tree in the backyard of their new blue house. "You two going to be okay back here?" he asked.

"Sure," said Charlotte, dangling Sock Monkey in front of Brandon's face. "Can I climb this tree?"

"Better not, if you want to get any peaches off of it," said Bart. "Holler if you need anything."

Charlotte looked up into the branches, counted the fuzzy green knobs that would be peaches some day, and smiled. Dumping Brandon's toys into the playpen, she watched him scramble for the ring-stack puzzle. "You know, kid, this is a great place," she said. "We'll have fresh peaches off our own tree this summer. I'll keep my bike in the shed, and I can get a cat. We'll play in the yard every day. You can mess up your own room as much as you want, and stay out of mine. How's that sound?"

"Big first," said Brandon, grubbing for stray plastic doughnuts among the toys around him.

"That's right," said Charlotte. Mom said if they all talked to Brandon as if he could understand, he'd learn to have real conversations. "The big green one. Where's that?"

Baby-sitting Brandon took only half Charlotte's brain as long as he was in the pen. She watched him work through the mysteries of the ring-stack puzzle, a frown of concentration on his face. She could barely remember what it was like to be little, to live in a mysterious world too big to take in all at once. Brandon had to focus tightly on one thing at a time in order to think at all. He couldn't daydream or plan, the way Charlotte could, about long hot summer afternoons playing in the shade of the peach tree. They'd swim at the municipal pool four blocks away.

When she felt like being alone, she'd leave Brandon with Bart, go into her room, and shut the door. When . . .

A door banged. Charlotte looked up. A girl carrying two plastic cups marched out of the house next door and up to the fence. "Hi," she said. "I'm Shannon Kohn. Want some lemonade?"

"Okay," said Charlotte. "I'm Charlotte Verstuyft." She walked over to the chain-link fence and took the sweating plastic cup offered to her. She and Shannon sized each other up. Charlotte was the shorter, but Shannon was the skinnier.

"Did you just come to town?" asked Shannon.

"No," said Charlotte. "We were in an apartment on the west side. But Mom got a job on this side of town. My stepdad's going to convert the garage into an office for his consulting business, and we'll save on day care for Brandon and rent on a storefront and everything's going to be so cool."

"Is Brandon your stepbrother?"

"Half brother. Bart and Mom got married ages ago."

Shannon waved at Brandon. He waved Sock Monkey back. "He's cute," she said. "I hope the ghost doesn't scare him."

Charlotte eyed Shannon suspiciously. "What ghost?"

"The one in your house," said Shannon, looking her straight in the eye.

"Ha-ha," said Charlotte, folding her arms. "This house isn't old enough to have a ghost."

"It's not so new. This whole subdivision was built right after World War II. That was a long time ago."

Nothing could be more ordinary than this subdivision of nearly identical houses on nearly identical cul-de-sacs. The casement windows of the back bedroom stood open wide, and Charlotte could see and hear the movers wrestling Mom and Bart's ordinary bed through the ordinary door. "Not long enough ago to make a ghost."

"You'll see," said Shannon. "Or maybe you'll hear. Little kids and animals can see her, but once you get older you can't."

"That's because she's not there," said Charlotte, tired of being polite about this.

"Is too," retorted Shannon. "I saw her. I was real little so I can hardly remember, but I threw a ball once and it landed under that tree right there, and I started to climb the fence, and I got my pants caught. And I started crying. And this girl came down out of the tree and brought the ball back and unhooked me from the fence. And then she disappeared."

"Yeah, right," said Charlotte, mashing down the uneasiness in her stomach. "What did she look like?"

"She had brown hair in a ponytail, and her dress was red, white, and blue stripes."

"I bet she was a regular girl."

"Then how did she disappear?"

"This is the biggest load of bull I ever heard," declared Charlotte loudly. "There's no such things as ghosts!"

"That's what Ms. Gonzalez said, the last lady that lived here," said Shannon, unfazed. "She took a year lease and left after six months. She had a baby, and he kept playing with somebody that wasn't there, and one day she found him hovering over his crib. Just floating in the air. So they packed up and left." Shannon lowered her voice and leaned over the fence. "Last Fourth of July, the house was empty. But I was lighting sparklers, and I looked over here, and I saw lights in the windows of the bedrooms." She pointed. The three bedrooms lined up, back to front, on the side of the house closest to Shannon's yard.

"Kids with flashlights," suggested Charlotte.

Shannon shook her head. "They were a funny kind of greenish light, and they bobbed around at the *tops* of the windows."

"You should have called the police," said Charlotte. "That's what I'd do. It was probably vandals."

Shannon didn't appear to be listening. "So—I figured—ghosts can't get you on the Fourth of July, right? That's the most unscariest holiday in the world. So I went up to the front window of that bedroom that looks onto the street."

"That's my bedroom," Charlotte informed her.

"Ooh, cool," said Shannon, "except I could never sleep there after what I saw."

"You didn't see a thing."

"I went right up to the window and put my face next to the glass," said Shannon, "and there was this light, bobbing around. Not a solid light, but like a shower of sparks, only they never went out. And suddenly it stopped and *swooped* right down at me; I mean straight at my face! And before I could back off, it came through the window and right through me! And it was *cold*! Like as if somebody spilled a bunch of ice water all over my molecules—inside ones, too! I was shivering and had goose pimples all up and down my legs, and it was still ninety degrees outside. So I *know* there's a ghost."

Charlotte opened her mouth to pour scorn on this story, and jumped as something thumped against her back. She whirled, her heart thumping. Brandon waved both hands at her. "Come play!" He smiled so sweetly it was impossible to be mad at him. Sock Monkey lay in a heap at her feet.

"Hey, he's got a great pitch," said Shannon.

"Yeah, Bart says he's going to be a baseball player," said Charlotte, picking up Sock Monkey. "I need to play with him now, or he'll get all whiny." Besides, if she played with Brandon, she wouldn't have to listen to Shannon's lies. They *had* to be lies.

She took a step closer to the playpen, away from the fence. But Shannon didn't take the hint. "Do you get paid to baby-sit?"

"No. Why should I? Mom didn't get paid to look after me."

"Mom says mothers should be paid because it's such an important job, and Dad says they should be paid *not* to have kids because of overpopulation. That's why I'm here, but I don't have any brothers and sisters, to satisfy both of them." She peered over the fence at Brandon, who waved the ring-stack puzzle by the base, scattering plastic doughnuts. "He's cute, in an obnoxious sort of way."

"Lottie play!" Brandon commanded.

"Want to help?" asked Charlotte, trapped.

"Okay," said Shannon, passing her cup over the fence and inserting one skinny bare foot into the chain link to hoist herself over. "But I don't know how much good I'll be."

"Lottie play!"

At least Shannon would be company. "Nothing to it," Charlotte assured her. "Just let him boss you around, and you'll be fine."

2

The New Family

Susie sat in the peach tree, watching the new girl get acquainted with the neighbor girl. She felt the warm bark of the tree and the stir of the breeze and saw the girls take the baby out of the playpen and clap patty-cake with him. But she had let her other senses drift away and couldn't hear the patty-cake rhyme or the rustling leaves, just the giggling of the little boy. A squirrel jumped from the live oak tree in the next yard onto the shed roof, braced himself to leap into the peach tree, and stopped to chatter at her; but she couldn't hear that, either. Susie stuck her tongue out at him.

Susie was disposed to like the new girl. She wasn't sharp or impatient with her little brother, and she seemed prepared to play his repetitive games all afternoon. She shared her lemonade, holding the cup so it didn't spill, and kept track of his explorations of the yard even while talking with the girl from next door. Susie knew—nobody better!—how tedious small children could be and how easy it was to look away from them when you shouldn't.

Not as tedious as being alone all the time, though.

Susie's vague, perpetual sense that she was waiting for someone formed unexpectedly into an unanswerable question: When would Mama, Daddy, and Gloria come back?

Her mind skittered away from the thought as the squirrel skittered away from her. Peacefully, she watched the shade of the peach tree stretch into midafternoon. The moving van went away. The little boy's walk became unsteady, so that he tripped and fell down every few minutes. The new girl returned him to the pen, settling him on his stomach. Nap time, thought Susie. The new girl rubbed his back until his eyes closed and his mouth relaxed, then moved a short distance away with the girl from next door. They started a hand-clapping pattern—"Under the Bamboo," Susie thought, from the motions.

Not very smart, thought Susie. What if the noise wakes him up? She drifted downward, feeling the scrape of the branch's molecules against her own, and lighted in the playpen, refocusing her ears just enough to keep track of the clapping game. Sitting cross-legged, she stroked the baby's back and sang softly:

"Nobody loves me, everybody hates me,
Guess I'll go into the garden to eat worms."

He stirred when the girls slapped their hands together in the big finish to "Under the Bamboo," but he didn't wake till the parents came out.

They were like all parents at this stage: big and loud and friendly to the neighbor girl. Suddenly the shade under the peach tree was crowded, too full of people for her to ignore the fact that she was being ignored. I'm so tired of this! Susie thought. How long will this go on?

How long *had* it been going on?

As always, when she thought about time, concentration became hard, so Susie drifted into the house to look around instead.

The only food in the kitchen so far was a box of cereal and a gallon of milk. Unopened cardboard boxes crowded the counter and table. In the living room, the furniture looked small and lost amid boxes labeled "Books," "Videos," and "Software." Susie, who had learned about videos several families ago, opened that box. Good—lots of cartoons and several movies she'd never seen. These people must be great TV watchers, because they had two sets—one large one, on an entertainment center opposite the picture window, and one smaller one, though still bigger than the one she'd pestered Daddy to buy. It was odd of the family to set up two TVs in one room, and even odder to put a flat typewriter keyboard in front of the smaller one. The TV—marked IBM—rested on top of what she at first took for a VCR, but its slots were too small for a videotape. Maybe it was one of the hi-fis—no, *stereos*—that played itty-bitty records.

It was too confusing. Susie lost interest and drifted to the bedrooms.

In her room at the front of the house, a bare twin bed, desk, dresser, and empty bookcase were ranged around the walls. In the middle of the floor stood three unpacked boxes marked: "Charlotte's Toys," "Charlotte's Clothes," and "Charlotte's Books & Stuff."

Charlotte. That was a nice name.

According to the boxes in Gloria's room, the baby's name was Brandon. Oh, well. She'd seen worse. Moving into the large back room, she learned the parents' names. Sylvia and Bart, huh! They sounded like kids to her, not grown-ups. And what was this—*another* TV? Didn't these people do anything else? Through the back window she could see the father play-wrestling Brandon. They all looked happy, enjoying one another's company. No one looked in her direction or showed any sign of knowing she existed. She jerked herself away from the sight, back to her own—Charlotte's—room.

Once, Susie had been shy about snooping into other people's things. Mama would say it was bad manners. But as people came and went, and Mama never returned, she cared less and less. The problem of not being able to get a grip on things had faded with practice. Now she knew how to focus her hands to open the boxes and dig through the contents. Charlotte's favorite color seemed to be yellow, and cats and butterflies decorated most of her things. Her books were the kind Susie liked herself—*Little Women,* Marguerite Henry, the Little House books, with some new paperback series about girls in clubs. Susie didn't know what to think when she found a Sega Genesis. Several video-game-playing boys had lived in her house, but she'd never thought of the games as a girl sort of thing.

Because she had forgotten to turn her ears on, Susie didn't hear Charlotte coming, and she jumped in surprise when the girl marched straight through her on the way to the boxes. Susie stepped aside and focused her ears.

"Hey!" Charlotte said. "How'd it get cold all of a sudden?" She rubbed the goose pimples out of her arms and knelt by the box of toys.

Susie drifted upward, out of the way, as Charlotte unpacked, putting butterfly sheets and a bedspread on her bed, then loading it with stuffed animals that she talked to cheerfully. "Sorry to leave y'all in the dark so long! But I had to look after Brandon." She held up a battered pink cat. "Mom says we'll go to Animal Control for a real kitten next week. But don't worry, Thomasina, I'll still love you!"

A real kitten! Susie sighed. She liked kittens, but they didn't like her anymore.

Charlotte gave no sign that she had heard. Susie hadn't expected one. As she hovered under the ceiling, the urge came over her to *make* her pay attention, though she had the feeling that she had done this before and had regretted it later. But listening to Charlotte chatter at the deaf toys, when Susie was right there, was almost unbearable. "Why are you talking to them?" she called down. "They can't hear you. And I can. This is *my* room, you know!"

"That girl Shannon's kind of weird," Charlotte informed the stuffed cat as she put her books in alphabetical order.

"Then don't be friends with her," said Susie loudly, coming lower. "*I'm* normal!"

"But it was nice of her to bring over lemonade. I couldn't tell if she was trying to scare me, or if she believed that stuff." Charlotte turned her back on the bookcase to cram her clothes all anyhow into the dresser and closet. "I don't care what she says, this place is too nice . . ."

Susie missed the rest of what Charlotte said because she was focusing on her hands. The paperback series on top of the bookcase was propped up by two bookends shaped like cats. A pull here, a push there, and the weight of the books did the rest, sliding sideways and tossing one bookend onto the floor. Charlotte whirled around at the sound. Susie focused quickly on her hearing, but all she heard was, "Shoot! I'm glad that didn't break!"

"I could have thrown it *at* you, you know," Susie pointed out.

Charlotte walked through her, shivering. Susie yelped and shot up out of her way. "Will you look where you're going? You burn, don't you know that?"

Charlotte hummed as she replaced the books and bookend. Forgetting about the half-unpacked clothes, she began thumbtacking cat and butterfly posters to the wall.

"Those things are bad for the wall," Susie said, but Charlotte paid no attention. Annoyed, Susie circled the room as fast as she could, raising a cool breeze that flapped the edges of the posters and blew Charlotte's hair into her eyes.

Charlotte tossed her head back and glared at the poster. "Stop that!"

"Make me!" Susie dropped suddenly, right next to her. "Or ask me politely! Or something!"

"Th-that's better." Charlotte glanced over her shoulder before inserting the next thumbtack. Susie passed her hand in front of her eyes.

"What do you expect to see back there? I'm right here!"

Something was wrong. Something was very wrong. (And hadn't it been wrong many times before?) Susie stared into Charlotte's eyes, willing her to speak. Charlotte seemed to be looking past her, at the poster; then her eyes shifted, and she was looking Susie straight in the eye. She opened her mouth. Hope stiffened Susie.

"Lottie!" Sylvia called from the hall. "Bart's going to McDonald's. You want a hamburger or McNuggets?"

Charlotte turned her back on Susie and went to the door. "McNuggets with sweet 'n' sour sauce."

Hopelessly, Susie drifted after her, letting her face break the surface of the wall above the door as it would break the surface of the water if she were backfloating. "I might be hungry, too, you know," she said.

"And can I have a milk shake?" asked Charlotte.

"I guess. You about settled in?"

Susie tried again. "Hello? You're in my house. You could think to offer me a milk shake."

"Yeah," said Charlotte, dashing forward to hug her

mother round the waist. “My room’s really cool, and there’s lots of space.”

“It’ll seem small enough in a year or two,” said Sylvia. “Compared to the place we used to have in Corpus—”

“Oh, I don’t care about that place! I don’t even remember it much. This house is perfect.” She hung on her mother and looked up. She seemed to be searching for a phrase that would express her enthusiasm. “I don’t *ever* want to leave!”

For some reason, the statement gave Susie a small chill, and she retreated, quickly, through the roof.

3

Who's Susie?

They went to Animal Control to get the new cat on Saturday.

Charlotte went in, excited, and came out with a stomachache. All those cats and dogs, most of them about to die in the gas chamber because she hadn't picked them! To keep herself from thinking about it, she talked to the single kitten she had been allowed to save—a half-grown tortoiseshell, with an alert, multicolored face. "What should I name you?" she asked it. "Rags? Raggedy Ann? Raggedy Muffin? Rag Rug?"

"She looks more like a crazy quilt," said Mom.

"Quilt's a stupid name," said Charlotte. "What's the other word for that?"

"Comforter? That's just as bad."

"No. Patchwork, that's it." She peered in through the slots in the side of the cat carrier. "Patchy? Is your name Patchy?"

"Prrp," said the kitten.

When they got home, Charlotte opened the carrier in the kitchen, where food and water bowls waited. Following Mom's advice, she didn't interfere as Patchy ventured out of the carrier, nose twitching, tail high. First the kitten hopped onto the windowsill and looked out. After satisfying herself that she had the lay of the land, she washed her stomach, then marched across the table to Charlotte and shoved her arm with her head. "Looks like she knows who she belongs to," said Bart. "Should she be on the table?"

"Keeping cats off furniture is more trouble than it's worth," said Mom. "As long as she stays off at mealtimes, that's all I ask. Is Brandon safe in his playpen?"

"Patchy wouldn't hurt him," said Charlotte.

"But he might hurt her," said Bart. "He's not old enough to know the difference between a live animal and a stuffed one. And you've seen how he treats his stuffed ones!"

Bart and Mom went about their business, but Charlotte watched Patchy eat—she purred like a refrigerator—and followed her as she explored the house. At the open door to Brandon's room, Patchy stopped short.

Her back arched.

Her ears went back.

"Hisss!" she said, and galloped away.

Charlotte could see Brandon's crib and the edge of the playpen, but not Brandon. When she poked her head in, Brandon looked up and took Sock Monkey's paw out of his mouth. "Susie Lottie *play*!" he commanded.

"Susie?" repeated Charlotte. "Who's Susie?"

"Susie Lottie play!" repeated Brandon, throwing Sock Monkey—not at Charlotte, but at a point inside the room.

"You better never throw things at my cat, squirt," said Charlotte, retrieving the toy. "I'll be right back, okay?"

Patchy was on top of the dishwasher, washing herself furiously, as if to force her fur to lie flat. Charlotte petted her and got grabbed by the wrist. "What scared you so bad?" Charlotte asked, wrestling her kitten gently.

"Mrrp," said Patchy.

Brandon and Patchy were formally introduced later that afternoon in the living room. Bart was playing Tetris, but Charlotte supervised the cat and Mom supervised the child, so they were well prepared for incidents. Patchy looked suspicious as Charlotte held her and Mom held Brandon's hand and guided him to pet her. "Gently," Mom cooed. "Gently. Just like that! Good boy!" But the kitten didn't hiss or bristle her fur, only moved her ears uneasily before relaxing and batting his hand with her paw, claws decently sheathed. Brandon giggled and tried to grab her, not knowing any better. Mom caught him, and Patchy slipped neatly away. With every action, she was proving herself to be a well-behaved and sensible cat, not the kind to hiss and run away from nothing—and yet she had.

"Mom," said Charlotte, "who's Susie?"

"I don't know," said Mom, restraining Brandon so he wouldn't chase after the cat.

"I've probably known a dozen in my lifetime," said Bart, over the click and rattle of keys, "but none of them are current. What about her?"

"Brandon asked for her earlier," said Charlotte.

"Really? Brandon, who's Susie?" Mom bent over him, making eye contact to make sure he paid attention.

"Susie flies," said Brandon, circling his hands in the air.

"There's your answer," said Bart. "She's a pretend friend."

"Isn't he young for pretend friends?" asked Charlotte. "I think I was three before I invented Dot-to-Dot Girl."

"If he has one, he must be old enough," said Mom. "Don't worry, this doesn't mean he's going to turn out smarter than you!"

"Dang!" said Bart. "Level nine beat me again!"

"My turn," said Charlotte. "I bet I can beat your high score this time." Tetris involved maneuvering computer-generated shapes so that they filled up the screen horizontally, with no gaps. It was a good game to play when something was bothering you, especially when, like now, you weren't sure that what was bothering you was real.

That night, Charlotte lured Patchy into her room and onto the bed. Their pleasant lights-out game of "mouse-under-the-covers" (Charlotte's hand playing the part of the mouse) ended abruptly when Patchy leaped straight up and turned in midair, landing braced to spring.

Charlotte laid her hand on the cat's back. "What *is* it?" she whispered. "What do you see?"

Patchy's fur bristled, but she didn't hiss or move, only stared at the cupboard above the closet. Charlotte stared, too. "What do you *see*? Is something in there?"

That was silly. Even if there were, cats didn't have X-ray eyes. Charlotte started to roll over, and thought she saw a shower of sparks falling across the darkness into the cupboard door.

Patchy's body and fur both relaxed.

"Is it gone?" Charlotte asked, but she knew the answer. She'd seen it go through the cupboard door.

It. Them. A shower of sparks. Like the ones Shannon had seen—said she had seen—in this room. They had come through the window at her.

If sparks could go through a door, they could go through a wall. Into Brandon's room.

Charlotte pulled her pillow over her head. "It's not a ghost," she whispered into the stuffy darkness. "Ghosts are dead people, and this is a kid ghost, and kids don't die."

Not usually. If they never did, there wouldn't be school safety films about how to avoid being hit by cars, or locked in old refrigerators and suffocated, or—

Charlotte yanked the pillow off her head, breathed deeply of the hot air, and got up. Mom and Bart were watching the news, so it was past ten. They couldn't be mad at her for getting up if all she did was check on Brandon on her way to the bathroom.

All looked peaceful by the dim, low glow of the dinosaur night-light. Charlotte peered over the edge of the crib. He'd be too big for it soon, but right now he was curled up in a thicket of stuffed animals, looking small and sweet and helpless, with his rump in the air. Charlotte reached in to resnap his pajama top to his pajama bottoms—

And gasped.

The cold spot vanished in the time it took her goose bumps to form. Charlotte felt the blanket, and it was cool.

But Brandon was warm and fast asleep.

4

The Story

Sunday, Shannon's parents invited them over to a cookout. Smoke hung in the air above the grill as the two families sat around the picnic table, passing the mustard and potato chips. Bart asked about the neighborhood. Mr. Kohn had lived here practically his whole life and had lots to tell—all boring as could be, Charlotte thought, but Mom and Bart seemed interested. "So is the neighborhood on the upswing now?" asked Mom, cutting up Brandon's hamburger.

"I think so," said Mr. Kohn. "And we're a community,

not just a bunch of houses. Our Fourth of July block party may not be as classy as the festivals the historic districts put on, but it's for us, not the tourists. San Antonio does too much for tourists and not enough for ourselves, that's what I say."

"A block party?" said Mom. "That wasn't in the real estate man's sales pitch."

"I don't know why not," said Mrs. Kohn. "It's the event of the year. The synagogue on the next street west and the Baptist church on the next street east club together for a sound system and a portable stage and put it up at the end of the cul-de-sac here. Everybody puts up tables and sets out food."

"Ice cream," said Shannon. "We provide the homemade kosher ice cream. And some girls in my summer school class are doing baton twirling, but I'm not coordinated enough."

"Well, count us in," said Bart. "I'll make my famous potato salad. This sounds like a neighborhood that's recovered, not recovering."

"I'd think the fact that you're buying your place proves we're out of the woods," said Mrs. Kohn. "That house was the first rental property in the area, and I swear nobody's ever lived there more than a year."

"That's because of the ghost," piped up Shannon.

"There's no such things as ghosts," said Charlotte's mom sharply.

"You'd be surprised how many people believe in Sparkler Susie," said Mr. Kohn. "The last renter only lasted six months, and left spouting wild stories about flying babies."

"Sparkler *Susie*?" Charlotte repeated, though her tongue felt suddenly heavy and unmanageable, as if it would have said something else if it could.

"Susie Miller was her real name. Our parents used to tell us about the little girl that died here as a cautionary tale, not a ghost story. But of course the kids figured if somebody'd died at a house, it must be haunted."

"It *is,*" said Shannon. "I've seen her. And so have you!"

"I used to say I had," said Mr. Kohn. "But all I really remember is seeing a girl with a ponytail when I was very small."

"But kids don't die," protested Charlotte.

"Not normally," said Mr. Kohn, apparently not noticing the frown Charlotte's mom directed at him. "There was an accident with a firework. My mother always said she blew her hands off, but I don't know if that's literally true, or just the kind of gory detail mothers tack on to make sure they make an impression."

"But fireworks are illegal inside the city," said Charlotte, over the small shocked noise her mom made.

"That doesn't keep people from using them," said Mr. Kohn.

"Charlotte's going to have nightmares tonight if we keep talking about this," said her mother.

"No, she won't," said Mr. Kohn. "This story's part of growing up around here—tradition. The block party's pretty much put an end to playing with fireworks, but I remember boys used to dare each other to hang on to them in the driveway of your house. Firecrackers, mostly. You'd hang on as long as you dared, and then drop them and run away screaming that Susie'd jerked it out of your hand."

"Your sister still swears that she *didn't* drop her firecrackers when she did it," Mrs. Kohn reminded him.

Mr. Kohn shrugged. "She's repeated the story so often, she's started to believe it."

"Just because a story's traditional doesn't mean it has to be repeated forever," said Charlotte's mom. "There's no such thing as ghosts. Why encourage the kids to believe in them?"

"I'm not sure there's no such thing," said Mrs. Kohn.

"And weird things happen in that house," said Shannon. "You'll see."

"I doubt it," said Bart. "Weird things don't happen to us."

"Um," said Charlotte.

"Oh, honestly!" exclaimed Mom.

"No, let her say," said Bart. "Otherwise she'll brood about it. What do you think you've seen, Lottie?"

Wishing she'd kept quiet, Charlotte stammered: "Like—do you ever get a cold draft?"

"Sure, when I'm sitting in front of the air conditioner."

"No, I mean, in the hall or one of the bedrooms. It always goes away real quick, but for a second it's like walking into a freezer."

"You're exaggerating," said Mom. "Some of the darker corners of the house are naturally cooler, but that's a good thing. You'll be grateful for it come July."

"And Patchy sees things that aren't there. You can see her looking at them, and her tail gets all puffed up."

Bart laughed. "I had a roommate for a while that had a cat, and I asked him once what the heck it was doing. Because it'd stare at this completely empty space in the middle of the room, lash its tail back and forth, settle down like it was going to pounce—you'd swear there was a mouse, but there never was. And he told me she was hunting invisible trolls."

"Trolls?" said Charlotte.

"So I said, 'But we don't have any trolls.' And he said, 'She does a good job, doesn't she?' "

The grown-ups laughed, but Charlotte noticed they hadn't explained anything. She decided not to mention the sparks. They'd probably tell her she'd been dreaming.

"I'll tell you the thing that bugs me about that story," said Shannon. "Was Susie too dumb to know to let go of the firework, or what?"

"I have no idea." Mr. Kohn helped himself to more potato chips. "She might have had a box, accidentally dropped the lighted punk in, and been grubbing around trying to get it out. Or she might have been playing with defective fireworks."

"I can't imagine how a mother could let that happen," said Sylvia, shuddering. "How can anybody let her kids run around unsupervised when there are explosives going off all around?"

As if on cue, Brandon hurled himself out of her lap toward a squirrel that swished its tail in the grass beyond the grill. By the time Mom stood up he was on the verge of running between the grill's legs, but Mr. Kohn, the closest, snatched him up and carried him, kicking and complaining, to the playpen.

"*That's* how," said Mrs. Kohn. "That's why I had only one kid. It lets me focus. You're terribly brave to have two, Sylvia."

"That's why I spaced them so far apart," said Charlotte's mom. "I didn't want a second little kid till the first one was old enough to know better. I can trust Charlotte."

It appeared that Mom had finally succeeded in changing the subject, and they started talking about babysitting, day care, new jobs, old jobs, and other yawnworthy subjects. Charlotte and Shannon licked the salt off their fingers and got off the picnic bench. First stop was Brandon's playpen.

"Has he seen her yet?" asked Shannon in a low voice.

"I'm . . . not sure," said Charlotte, with the uncomfortable feeling that she was lying. "He has a pretend friend named Susie."

"Susie fly," Brandon informed them, throwing Sock Monkey at a squirrel.

Charlotte retrieved the toy and held it up just out of reach. "What's she like?" she asked him. "Is she cold?"

Brandon grabbed futilely at Sock Monkey. "Worms," he said.

"What?" Shannon and Charlotte chorused.

"Worms," said Brandon, taking advantage of Charlotte's distraction to seize Sock Monkey. "Sing worms!"

"I know a song about worms," said Shannon. "We sing it at school." She glanced sideways at the grown-ups, bent over the playpen, and crooned:

"The worms crawl in and the worms crawl out;
They play pinochle on your snout.
They invite their friends, and their friends' friends, too,
And you look like heck when they're through with you!"

"That is so gross!" Charlotte complained. "Don't put ideas into his head!"

"Too late," said Shannon. "Susie's already doing it. Hey, Brandon!" She snapped her fingers to distract him from the project of inserting Sock Monkey's head into his mouth. "Brandon! Is this what Susie sings? '*The worms crawl in and—*' "

Charlotte clapped a hand over Shannon's mouth. Brandon only regarded her blankly. "No Susie," he said. "Ulp worms."

"Oh, that makes gobs of sense," said Charlotte.

Shannon wrinkled her forehead wisely, pulling Charlotte's hand away. "It probably does if you're two. I'll tell you something for sure—Sparkler Susie likes little kids. The grown-ups never see her. Kids do sometimes, but there's *always* something going on with the babies."

"If she likes them, she wouldn't . . . hurt them. Would she?"

"Not on purpose, I guess," said Shannon. "And there wasn't anything gross or scary about her when she helped me over the fence. But—heck—she's a ghost. Who knows what she'd do? And what's the deal with the worms? That's what I want to know."

Charlotte nodded. "Me, too!"

"We'll have to ask her."

"How?" asked Charlotte. "We can't even see her."

"We'll hold a séance."

Charlotte had heard the word in a movie once, one that was too scary to watch to the end. "You mean where you sit around a table with the lights out and call up the spirits? Don't you need a lot of people for that?"

"Naw," said Shannon. "See, some people are mediums,

and they have this natural talent for getting in touch with ghosts. The medium calls and they come, or she goes into a trance and the ghost takes over her body and talks through her."

"Ick," said Charlotte. "I'm glad I'm not one!"

"You might be," said Shannon. "Or I might, since I've seen her twice."

"Well, if you want to be a medium, you go ahead," said Charlotte. "I'm sure I'm not one."

"I tried being one at a Halloween party last year, and all that happened was my legs fell asleep from sitting cross-legged. But maybe there weren't any ghosts at Ashleigh's house."

The idea that maybe none of this would work made Charlotte feel better. "I'll ask if you can come over after supper tonight. Maybe you'll see how Patchy acts, anyway."

5

A Séance

"Sing worms," said Brandon.

"Only if you close your eyes and lie still," said Susie.

Brandon promptly closed his eyes and laid his head on his arm. Susie, hovering above and parallel to him, stroked his back and sang: "Nobody loves me, everybody hates me . . ." He giggled when she swallowed the worms and again when she urped them up, but as she sang the song through again and again and again, stroking his back, he gradually stopped reacting. She had done this so often, with so many children, that she recognized the instant in which he fell asleep.

Susie sighed and stretched, floating above the crib. She had lost track of how many children she had taken care of while waiting for her family. Animals avoided her. People older than Gloria ignored her. Small children enabled her to keep from wondering if, perhaps, she weren't really here at all. But oh, how she wished she had someone her own age to do things with! She'd had friends once and had moved away from them. Mama had promised she'd make new friends. Well, where were they?

Susie focused her energy away from the thought and into her ears. Sylvia and Bart were watching a rerun in the living room. Shannon and Charlotte were moving around in Charlotte's bedroom, talking.

"So which of us should be the medium?"

"I don't think that's the sort of thing you can decide. We'll both sit here, holding hands to make an energy circle, and open ourselves up."

"Open ourselves how?"

"Just . . . open up your soul. You know."

"No, I don't."

"Look, if you're too chicken to do this, speak up."

"No. No, I can . . . I can try." Susie's hearing was so well tuned she could hear the girls' breathing. "Should we . . . call her or something?"

"Couldn't hurt." Twin deep breaths. Then the girls'

voices oozed out in unnatural, elongated tones: "Suuuu-usie. Suuuuusie. We're waiting for you."

Susie's heart jumped.

"Suuuusie. Suuuusie. Suuuuuusie."

It might be a trap, calling her so they could pick on her. But Susie didn't think Charlotte was like that.

"Suuuuusie. Suuuuusie. Please come talk to us."

And even being picked on would be better than being ignored! Shifting some of her energy into sight, Susie drifted through the cupboards above the closets and looked down at Charlotte's room.

The girls had closed the curtains and turned off the lights, but this didn't hinder Susie's ability to see. They sat cross-legged on the floor, facing each other, holding hands, eyes shut tight, heads tilted back. Patchy sprawled across the foot of Charlotte's bed. "Suuuusie," crooned the girls.

"I'm here," said Susie. "What do you want?"

Patchy woke up all at once, in the abrupt manner of a startled cat, but Charlotte and Shannon kept crooning her name. "Please contact us. We're waiting to speak to you."

"I'm here already!" Susie swooped down, and Patchy watched with wide, pupil-filled eyes, twitching her tail. "What's the matter with you? You deaf?"

"Suuuusie," moaned Charlotte.

Impatiently, Susie thrust herself straight through her.

Patchy hissed.

Charlotte's eyes flew open. "Did you feel that?"

"Feel what?"

"The cold spot!" said Charlotte, as Susie wheeled and thrust herself through Shannon, too.

Shannon jumped and shuddered. "Ew! It's like having ice cubes pushed through your skin! And look at Patchy!"

"Pffft!" said Patchy, crouching low on the bed and lashing her tail.

"Shut up, cat," said Susie, hovering over the bed. "I never did anything to you!"

Charlotte and Shannon looked straight at Susie. "What is it, Patchy? What do you see?" Charlotte whispered urgently.

"Me!" shouted Susie, waving her arms and bobbing up and down. "You wanted me, you got me! What do you want? What's the matter with you?"

Patchy hurled herself from the bed to the door, stretching to scratch at the knob. "Patchy, stop that!" said Charlotte. "I can't let you out now. If I let go of Shannon's hands, it'll break the energy circle."

"That noise'll break our concentration, anyway," said Shannon. "Maybe if we walked over there holding hands—"

"Oh, for heaven's sake," said Susie, shooting across the room and concentrating on her hands so that she could turn the knob. Patchy ran out as soon as a crack appeared, and Susie shut it after her, then turned and settled to the floor, her back against the door. Shannon and Charlotte stared at her.

"Su-susie?" Charlotte's voice sounded small and thin. "Is that you?"

"Of course it's me," Susie snapped.

"Show yourself to us," said Shannon. "Or you can . . . you can take over my body and use it to talk."

"Can't you see me?" Something clicked in Susie's head. Could she be invisible? So many confusing things would be explained if that were true! Why hadn't she thought of it before? (*Hadn't* she thought of it before? She had a vague sense of having thought, or almost thought, many things, but there was no time to sort it out now.) If she could touch things only by focusing her hands, and could shift her senses around by focusing on different ones—maybe she needed to focus in order to be visible!

It was worth a try.

Susie's hands were already concentrated enough to open doors, so she focused on them. The girls were still talking, but pouring all her energy into her hands meant her hearing and sight faded, so that they seemed to be far away, and their faces disappeared altogether. Just when Susie felt she didn't have an ounce more energy to use, Charlotte gasped. "Do you see that? Hands! They're reaching for us!"

"Hush," squeaked Shannon. "They're just hovering there. They won't hurt us. You won't hurt us, will you, Susie?"

Susie yanked all the energy in her hands up to her head and throat, realizing that she probably needed her vocal cords focused in order to be heard. "Of course not," she said.

Charlotte's freckles stood out like ink spatters on her white, scared face. "What . . . what do you want?" she asked.

"I want Gloria and Mama and Daddy to come back," said Susie, feeling the vibrations in her vocal cords. Her face was uncomfortably warm, and her whole self felt strained. "I'm tired of being ignored in my own house!"

"But it's not your house," said Charlotte, her voice fading in and out. "It's our house now."

"We want to help you," said Shannon, but her next sentence was garbled. Susie's eyes swam. One moment the girls and the room were sharply clear, the next they blurred and faded.

"I don't need any help," said Susie. "I'll be fine when my folks come back. In the meantime, Brandon's all the company I have! I like Brandon, but you can only take little kids for so long." She couldn't tell if she was still audible, couldn't tell if her fierce concentration on her head did any good.

The girls spoke, their voices stretched and unintelligible, like a record played on the wrong speed. "Brandon . . . here . . . who . . . Gloria?"

Susie drew closer, trying to listen, trying to speak clearly, though her mouth felt like mush. "Gloria, my sister," she said. "Gloria Miller. She's five. Mama and Daddy took her somewhere. Can you hear me? I can't hear you." She groped, forgetting that her hands weren't concentrated, forgetting what she was doing as her grip upon her energy loosened and let her fall apart.

6

The Absent Ghost

"Well," said Shannon as Charlotte turned the lights on, "I didn't see any worms."

Charlotte shuddered, rubbing her arms. "I wish we had! Seeing her whole body with worms coming in and out would've been better than just those hands—and just that face! Eeuw!"

"You wouldn't say that if you'd seen it," said Shannon, scribbling in a notebook. "It would have been major gross."

"But it wouldn't have been *scary,*" said Charlotte, turning on the desk lamp, opening the closet, and switching on that light, too. "What do you think she meant about Brandon?"

"I don't know," said Shannon. "It was like watching cable TV on a scrambled channel."

"And listening to the radio when the station won't tune," agreed Charlotte. "What are you writing?"

Shannon passed her the notebook. "Is that about what you heard her say?"

Charlotte read:

I want Gloria and Mama and Daddy to come back. I'm tired of being ignored in my own house! Help . . . find my folks. I've come back . . . Brandon's . . . company . . . ! I like Brandon, but . . . take . . . so long . . . Gloria, my sister . . . Gloria Miller. She's five. Mama and Daddy took her.

A knock on the door made them both jump. "Girls," called Charlotte's mom. "Mrs. Kohn wanted Shannon home by eight-thirty."

"Coming!" called Shannon. She tapped the page with the pencil point. "You need to study on this. She wants us to find her family, and she won't rest till we do."

Charlotte swallowed. "O-okay."

"And don't be scared! She's a ghost, not a monster."

But knowing that Susie could be anywhere, and that

Charlotte wouldn't know the difference, made the small of her back feel continually creepy and exposed. Whenever she blinked, she saw those hands, stretching out through the darkness, lit by a pale glow, or that face—such an ordinary face, except that it had no body and flickered as its lips moved. The images were no more solid than the patterns of light that made up a TV picture, she thought; but something about Susie was solid enough to open doors. Should she tell Mom and Bart? Would anything have convinced *her* that ghosts were real if she hadn't seen that hovering face? She went to bed still holding the secret tight.

The night was too hot to have the covers on, but she felt bare and exposed without them, so she kept pulling them up and pushing them off again. Even with her closet light on, there was too much darkness in the room.

I've come back. Help. Find my folks!

How could she help somebody she couldn't even talk to?

Brandon's company. Take so long.

And what did Brandon have to do with anything?

Tired of being ignored in my own house!

"Susie? I didn't mean to ignore you. Honest."

What if that face appeared, floating at the foot of the bed?

Ten o'clock. She heard Mom and Bart going to bed.

What was there to do at night if you were a ghost?

Did you ever sleep? Did you sleep in the daytime? Where and when *would* a ghost sleep?

Ten oh one.

What kind of person was Susie, anyway? Mean, nice, smart, dumb—what? What about that kid Shannon'd said she levitated? Was that just playing, or had she been about to carry it off?

Carry it off where?

What did worms have to do with anything?

Ten oh two.

The door creaked.

Charlotte tried to say Susie's name, but her mouth was dry and she wasn't breathing. She had heard of people dying of fright. Was this what it was like? Did you suffocate because you forgot how to breathe? Would she be a ghost, too, stuck here forever while her family moved on?

"Prrp," said Patchy, jumping onto the bed.

Charlotte relaxed and swallowed. "Patchy," she called softly, rolling onto her side and patting the bed next to her. "Come lie down by me. You'll let me know if that nasty old ghost comes!" she whispered.

Patchy walked the length of the bed and shoved her head against Charlotte's face, as if assuring her that things would look better in the morning.

And they did, though Charlotte had a hard time getting out of bed after lying awake till past midnight. It was Mom's first day back to work, and the new house was full of the ordinary frantic hurry of getting her out the door. Workmen showed up to start converting the garage into an office. Every corner of the house was unrelentingly hot by midmorning, except for the living room, where Bart worked on the computer. Charlotte ran electric fans in every room and tensed with fear every time Brandon asked for Susie, but she felt no cold drafts. Saw no ghostly hands. Heard no whispered voices.

Charlotte itched to consult Shannon, but she was at summer school—not because she would be held back without it, but because she was a brain and her folks wanted her to skip a year. As soon as Charlotte saw Shannon walking down the street, swinging her book bag, she got permission to run next door and ask her to go swimming.

"I think the séance got rid of Susie," she said as Shannon unlocked her front door.

"Séances don't work that way," said Shannon.

Although Charlotte had thought she wanted Shannon's opinion, the tone in which she said this made her bristle. "You don't know everything."

"I do about this." Shannon said calmly. "Or anyway, I know more than you do. Come in while I'm getting my suit on, and I'll show you how I know."

Shannon's room was cluttered with books, CDs, and electronics. She pointed at the bookcase by her bed as she kicked off her sandals and began rummaging through drawers. Battered books about weird things crammed the whole top shelf. "I've read every one of those. Sometimes twice. Plus stuff from the library. I know a *lot* about ghosts, and séances don't make them go away unless you send them to the light. They usually have unfinished business and don't know they're dead."

"How can they possibly not know they're dead?" Charlotte picked gingerly at the assortment. *Unexplained!; Encyclopedia of Ghosts; Facts, Frauds, and Phantasms; When Darkness Falls; Spirits of San Antonio and South Texas; Strangest of All.* If Mom ever saw these, she'd have three kinds of fit.

"I guess it's hard to think once your brain's not with you anymore," said Shannon. "I think it must be like dreaming, where time and space don't work right, but it all seems normal while you're in it."

"Or maybe it's like being little again. Maybe the reason she likes little kids is they've got the same attention span."

"Whatever, you have to finish their unfinished business, convince them they're dead, and help them find the light. Which is heaven or something, I guess; they're kind of vague about it in the books."

"You may know a lot of stuff out of books, but I'm the one who's been in the house all day, and Susie's not in it," Charlotte declared, becoming confident as she spoke. "Brandon can't see her anymore. She's gone."

"It's probably only temporary. Life is so unfair," said

Shannon, producing a red-and-white swimsuit that Charlotte privately thought was going to make her look like a candy cane. "I'd love to be haunted."

"No, you wouldn't," Charlotte declared. "It's no fun to have people's heads floating around your bedroom. I'm going to go swimming and forget all about it."

It was easy to forget at the pool, amid the confusion of bright suits, blinding reflections off the water, shouting children, and the definitive summer smells of chlorine and suntan lotion. And at home, even after nightfall and into the next days, everything was as normal as could be—Mom and Bart working while Charlotte baby-sat, watched TV, and played with Patchy, who never hissed and arched her back at "nothing" anymore.

Brandon got so bad about throwing stuff that Bart had to spank him a couple of times, and he took to running around the house at bedtime. "Where's Susie?" he'd shout. "Want Susie to sing worms!"

"We don't *have* Susie," Mom would say. "Maybe she'll come after you settle down and think about her for a while."

This got him into the crib the first couple of times, but he was soon standing up again, hollering for her to "sing worms." "Ignore him." Mom sighed, turning up the TV louder. "At this point, even spanking him counts as a reward, because as long as we respond to him, he doesn't have to go to sleep. Sooner or later, he'll grow out of this."

"Woooorms!" howled Brandon.

"What's the deal with the worms, though?" asked Bart.

"I have no idea."

Charlotte tried to get him to sing worms for her, hoping to learn it, but he ran the words together so fast she couldn't make sense of them. Nor could he explain about Susie. She came from the ceiling, but he didn't know where she had gone, and he wanted her back.

"What if *I* went away?" asked Charlotte after three days of this. "Would you fuss this much about me?"

"No!" said Brandon, throwing Sock Monkey at her.

"Then I'd better leave," said Charlotte, marching out. But she didn't go far. She stood in the hall where she could see him in the mirror over the dresser, and when his face crumpled up, she poked her head back in. "I'll come back if you say you're sorry and don't throw things anymore."

"Sorry," said Brandon in a small voice, holding his hands out to her. "Want Lottie *and* Susie."

"You'll have to settle for me and Sock Monkey," said Charlotte, folding him in a hug.

But by Sunday, when they invited the Kohns over for a cookout at their new picnic table, Brandon still missed Susie, and Charlotte had become convinced that her fear had been misplaced. The poor girl couldn't have been all that scary if he'd gotten this attached to her in such a short time.

"She'll be back by the Fourth of July," Shannon predicted confidently as they carried paper plates into the backyard. "That's her anniversary. Ghosts can go away in between times, but on their anniversaries, they have to show up. Whether they want to or not!"

"What a bummer," said Charlotte, not believing her.

7

Shadows of Light

Susie awoke floating before the door in Charlotte's empty bedroom. For a minute or two, she was confused, but this had happened before. The last time had been when she picked up the crying Gonzalez baby, intending to walk him around the room till he fell asleep. The woman's screams had scattered her, and she had collected herself again in an empty house.

Whenever someone over five noticed her, there was always a ruckus that left gaps in her life. Yet she always forgot in a few days, she realized, always began to long to be noticed, forgetting that if she did she would not be treated normally.

At least Charlotte and Shannon had talked to her. Maybe this time would be different.

Had she ever thought that before?

At least Charlotte's room still had all of Charlotte's stuff in it. The perpetual humming of the air conditioner in the living room told her that the house, though quiet, was not deserted. Susie drifted down the unlighted hall, past the closed door of the living room. All the windows in the rest of the house stood open, letting in daylight, the songs of birds, the moan of a passing car. In the back bedroom, she heard voices outside and smelled grilling burgers. The family sat around a new picnic table as smoke from a grill wrinkled the evening air.

Susie hadn't had a hamburger in ages.

Come to think of it, she hadn't eaten anything in ages.

The thought slid out of her head again as, not bothering with doors, Susie passed from the bedroom to the eternally cool living room. The family left the air on constantly because of the computer. Susie had almost forgotten that a few weeks ago she had thought of this as a TV. The memory of her ignorance hovered in the fog in the back of her brain, with all the other memories she never looked at.

The computer screen showed a yellow field across which red letters floated: GET BACK TO WORK!!! Susie nudged the oval device—the "mouse," of all the silly names—that Bart used to manipulate images on the screen. The screen saver gave way to the desktop. She moved the mouse till the arrow on the screen pointed at the Games symbol, then clicked the button. The machine thunked to itself a couple of times, as if it were thinking, then gave her a choice of games. Susie picked Tetris, which she had watched Bart and Charlotte play and thought she understood.

Slowly at first, then faster, shapes fell from the top of the screen. Slowly at first, then faster, Susie moved them with the arrow keys, rotated them, made them fall into the proper places. She focused her senses down to sight and hearing, so she could watch the shapes and hear the *boing* as they landed. Her sense of touch was limited to the pressure of her fingers on the keys. The first game went quickly—nine hundred eighty-nine points. Second game—twelve hundred sixteen points. Third game—fifteen hundred thirty-two points. Fourth game—

This was nothing; this was stupid; this didn't compare to playing dolls or hand-clapping games or house or softball or Chutes and Ladders or *anything* played with another person!

But the falling shapes went where she told them to go, responding without having to see her or know anything about her. Not like Charlotte.

Three thousand nine points. Hit the F2 key, start over.

Why could Brandon see her when Charlotte and Shannon could see only part of her, only when she focused impossibly hard?

When was the last time she had eaten?

How long did Mama and Daddy and Gloria plan on staying away?

And why had they left her here, all by herself?

The neglected memories and questions bubbled in the back of her head, but her eyes followed the falling shapes. Her fingers flew faster and faster to catch them, move them, make them vanish off the bottom of the screen as more shapes fell to replace them from the top. Where did they come from? What happened when they vanished? The shapes were only patterns of colored light, not real, yet she could see them. *Everybody* could see them.

Susie was real, yet hardly anybody could see her.

Six thousand seventeen points. She was invisible, but she could still learn things, still do things, even if only silly things like Tetris. F2. Start again.

Only the outermost edges of Susie's attention noticed the room dimming. The games flashed by. Seven thousand points, eight thousand points, nine thousand—faster, faster, faster, her fingers moved, as if the thought of motion didn't have to pass through muscle to become real. Somewhere on this machine was a screen where the names of the people with the ten highest Tetris scores were stored. If she could get onto that screen, put her name where everyone could see it—

Then what?

Nine thousand five hundred points. F2. Try again.

The world narrowed to the size of a computer screen and a keypad. Her sight saw nothing else; her ears heard nothing else; her sense of touch felt nothing else as the room darkened. Her brain was numb, all the bubbling thoughts shoved away, until something searingly hot passed through her. The screen blanked out, and Charlotte's voice said, inside Susie's ear, "It's okay. I've reset it."

The machine beeped and hummed.

"This is too weird," said Bart. "I'd better run a diagnostic."

Susie, dazed, moved out of his way before he sat down in the middle of her. Charlotte said to Bart, her eyes sliding over the room as if looking for something, "I'm going to call Patchy. I think she's in the backyard."

Susie hurled herself after Charlotte as she headed for the back door, past a table piled high with remains of the cookout. "What did you do that for?" she demanded, the possible consequences of being noticed already forgotten. "I was having a good game! I don't interrupt your games, do I? I've got rights in this house, too, you know!" She put her mouth as close to Charlotte's hot ear as she could and shouted, "This is my house, not yours! You can't push me around!"

Charlotte shivered, looked over her shoulder, opened the back door, and called, "Paaatchy! Kitty kitty kitty!"

Patchy bounded across the dark yard, stopping at the long rectangle of light falling out of the back door. Charlotte's shadow was black and fuzzy on the grass beyond the step. Susie's was not.

Why had she never noticed before that she had no shadow?

Patchy crouched at the edge of light, her eyes huge and black in her triangular face. She held her head low, swiveled her ears, lashed her tail.

"She's right behind me, isn't she, Patchy?" said Charlotte. Susie felt the other girl's body brace itself, as if for impact, before she turned her head. Her face was practically inside of Susie's, and goose pimples rose on her cheeks. "Susie. Come with me. I want to talk to you."

Charlotte stepped outside, holding the door open. Politely. No one had been polite to Susie since . . . since . . .

Patchy continued to crouch low in the grass until Susie stepped outside. Then the kitten dashed past her into the house. Charlotte closed the screen door, but not the inner one, so that the light still lay upon the grass. Then she sat down cross-legged, holding out her hand.

"Su-susie? I can't tell where you are. T-touch me, so I'll know."

Susie settled next to her, feeling the grass blades prickle in her legs, and reached out a hand. When her focused fingertips touched Charlotte's, a hot shiver ran through her. Charlotte shivered, too, the fine hairs standing up on her bare arms. "I hate this," she whispered.

"I don't like it either," said Susie. "What do you want?"

"But it's worse for you, isn't it? Listen. You said you wanted your folks to come back. Your mama and daddy and Gloria." Charlotte took a deep breath. "Have you got any idea how long it's been since they left?"

"A long time," said Susie impatiently. Too soon, too fast! Memory, not yet buried under a deep enough layer of distractions, stirred menacingly in response. "What difference does it make?"

"This is going to sound stupid, but it's true. Just listen. They've been gone for more than fifty years."

"You're right," said Susie loudly, trying to drown out the alarm bells ringing in the back of her head. "That's stupid!"

"They didn't want to leave you," Charlotte continued. "They didn't even know you were here. See—oh, drat. Shannon says you haven't figured this out, but I don't see how you can't have. Look around you! Everything's changed! Was there even a peach tree here when you came? Haven't there been a gazillion people living here since your folks left? Haven't all the cars changed, and the clothes, and—and everything? Had you even *heard* of computers when they left?"

Susie's senses trembled. She didn't have to listen to this. It was all true, but it didn't make any difference. It didn't. It didn't. If fifty years had passed, then she would have grown up. She'd be an old lady, and she wasn't. She was Susie Miller, ten years old, waiting for her family. It had been a while since they'd left, but it hadn't been *that* long.

It couldn't have been.

"Everything's changed but you," said Charlotte. "Haven't you ever wondered how that could happen?"

"No," said Susie. "No, no, no, no, because it isn't true!" She wanted to snatch her hand away from Charlotte's, fly up into the peach tree and beyond—but she didn't.

"I'm not saying this to be mean," said Charlotte, "even if it is a pain that my own brother likes you best. But you can't hang around here forever, Susie. Pay attention and *think*. Is there really anything here that you still want?"

"You don't understand. I *can't* go anywhere else." Except—maybe—straight up or straight down, which got her where?

"I belong here till Gloria comes back," said Susie. "I promised! And you are too being mean! You're a selfish, stupid girl that doesn't want to share!"

"Because you're not living here, Susie," said Charlotte

as if she couldn't hear what Susie had said, and probably she couldn't, Susie realized, because she wasn't focused. Charlotte couldn't see her, couldn't hear her, was sitting here bravely talking to empty air, because . . . because . . . because . . .

"You're haunting here," said Charlotte gently. "You're a ghost, and you've been dead for a long, long time."

8

Crying

The cold at the tips of Charlotte's fingers snatched itself away, and a trail of sparks showered across the yard into the peach tree. Charlotte stared as the sparks faded. She drew up her knees and hugged them, hunching her shoulders.

She made herself sit there for a while, in case Susie came back, fighting the urge to go inside and watch videos. Normal sunshiny videos about girls who went horseback riding or did gymnastics. It was bad enough trying to think about things like being dead, or being blown up by fireworks—her brain winced away from those ideas like a tongue from a canker sore—without having to think about being alone for fifty years, with only little kids for company.

Mom's shadow moved across the light from the kitchen windows. Pressing her hand in the small of her back, Charlotte went inside.

"Did Brandon go to bed okay?" she asked.

"He was worn out," said Mom, putting the three-liter soda bottle back in the refrigerator door. "You want a drink before you take your bath?"

Charlotte shook her head. "The Tetris game was playing itself."

"Yeah, Bart told me. He's in there running the diagnostic."

"It was kind of spooky," said Charlotte in a false, bright voice. "I think I'll tell Shannon the ghost was doing it."

"I wish you and Shannon didn't talk about the ghost," said Mom. "It's not healthy to think about that kind of stuff. And remember, Brandon understands more than he can say."

"But he doesn't know what being dead is about," said Charlotte.

"No, and I'd rather he didn't figure it out," said Mom. "He's too young for that sort of thing. So are you. So am I, as a matter of fact. Time enough to think about death when you're old enough to do it."

Was that Susie's problem, Charlotte wondered—too young to die, to think about death, and dead anyway? Charlotte wanted to tell her mom about the cold spot, about the séance, about Patchy, about the trail of sparks shooting off to the peach tree. But how could she when Mom didn't want to know? "If there *were* a ghost," she said, "it would be awful to be her."

Mom hugged her. "But there aren't any ghosts," she said, "so you don't need to worry about it. Go take your bath, and then you can sit up for a while reading one of your Little House books or something. That'll make you feel ordinary again."

So Charlotte tried, but the creepy feeling lingered. What if, while she brushed her teeth, a face formed beside hers in the mirror? What if Susie were hacked off at being told she was dead? What if fifty years of being alone had driven her crazy?

Charlotte tried reading *Little House on the Prairie,* but there were more scary parts in it than she had remembered: the fever and ague, the chimney that caught fire, the fear that the Indians would kill them. Of course, it turned out that the Indians had a right to be annoyed, because the family had built its little house in the wrong place. They were trespassing.

Just like Susie felt Charlotte's family was trespassing in her house. Which was true, as far as it went. If a house got to be more yours the longer you stayed in it, which made sense, no one would ever own this house more than Susie. But what good did it do her?

Charlotte wasn't aware of when she fell asleep, but when she woke, someone was crying.

Naturally, she thought first of Brandon, but Brandon cried like a baby still, high and whining and piercing, and this was so soft she could barely hear it. The door to her room had swung wide enough for her to see the living room door standing open to blackness. No light came from Mom and Bart's room. She looked at her clock. Three in the morning.

Patchy sat straight up on the foot of the bed, ears pricked forward, tail twitching.

"Is it her?" Charlotte asked, putting her hand on the cat's back. *Thud thud thud* went Patchy's heart.

Charlotte knew she should get up and find out what was wrong, but her legs felt like lead and her body like a block of wood. She had used up her bravery talking to Susie in the backyard. The sobs drifted through the house, sounding now as if they came from the living room, now from Brandon's room, distant and then near. Once or twice she thought the sound had stopped, and her eyes began to close, but then she'd hear a gasp, and it would start up again. Once or twice she thought she saw a trail of sparks cross the hall, but her eyes were so dry with straining to see that she couldn't be sure. She kept waiting for the sound to drift into her room, for Patchy's tense anticipation to turn into arched back and hissing. After an eternity or so, the sound changed, gained rhythm, gained words:

"Nobody loves me, everybody hates me,
I'm going to the garden to eat worms.
Ulp! goes one! Ulp! goes two! Ulp! goes number three!"

What in the world?

The voice took a ragged breath.

"Nobody loves me, everybody hates me.
I'm going to the garden to eat worms."

Charlotte wanted to call out: "I don't hate you. I'm just scared of you."

But her tongue lay in her mouth, too heavy to speak.

Dead, thought Susie, crying uncontrollably, as she had cried without knowing why on that first dreadful day, when she had first failed (or refused?) to realize what had happened to her. She was dead, and a ghost, and that explained everything.

Explained everything, and made no sense. She wasn't

supposed to be dead. She was only ten years old! She didn't remember dying (an echo of pain ran through her, and she focused away from it before she noticed herself noticing). She didn't know *how* to be dead. Weren't there supposed to be angels or something, to show her the ropes?

What were the rules?

Who made them?

She had promised to stay here, and the universe was enforcing her promise. Dashing out of the house in a shower of sparks, she hurled herself again and again at the property boundaries, but there was no way out. There never was any way out. No hope of release, but to forget again—she was good, she realized, at forgetting, at not noticing, at not knowing what it was unbearable to know. She could exist from day to day with false hope.

But not yet. Not quite yet, not if she could help it. Not with Charlotte in the house, treating her as someone real. Believing in her, as no one else would—except for the next small child, and the next, and the next. Charlotte wasn't likely to let her forget.

Everything was a mess, and there was no way out.

Was being noticed worth the pain of remembering all the time?

9

The Baby-sitters

Did you hear anything last night?" Charlotte asked, lifting Patchy away from her cereal bowl and setting her on the floor.

"Like what?" asked Mom, stirring her coffee.

"I thought I heard somebody crying," said Charlotte.

Mom and Bart shook their heads, and Brandon, with a crow of delight, threw his sippy cup at the window.

Now that the bright, hot day had begun, it bothered Charlotte that she had not tried to do something for Susie.

If she were brave enough to talk to a ghost, holding its coldly intangible hand, why hadn't she been brave enough to get up and look for her? Since she had done one, surely she could have done the other.

She worried about it all day as she and Brandon played and watched TV in the bedrooms, Bart worked on the computer, and the workmen made a hideous racket in the garage. Brandon kept wanting to play outside, but both the front and back garage doors stood open, and power tools were all over the place. Charlotte was exhausted by ten o'clock.

Back in his room, Brandon got into one of his throwing moods. He threw everything within reach—Sock Monkey, plastic doughnuts, beanbags—and he wasn't playing catch, either! When she tossed something gently back at him, he'd ignore it and hurl something with all his force at her. "Dang it, Brandon!" snapped Charlotte, dodging a Nerf football. "Why can't you play nice?"

"Don't wanna!" said Brandon, picking up the stick for the doughnut puzzle.

"No," said Charlotte, moving toward him to take it away, but he dodged her, giggling as he wound up for the throw. "No!"

He threw.

Charlotte, trapped between the crib and the wall, realized she had nowhere to dodge and it would hurt when it hit.

The stick stopped in midair, hovering three feet from Charlotte's face.

Charlotte stared. Brandon clapped. "Susie!"

The stick landed on the floor as if carelessly tossed aside, and Brandon, face shining like the sun, held his arms out to nothing. Charlotte could see his shirt hike up where Susie grabbed him, but she could not see the hands that scooped him through the air and dumped him into the crib. Staticky, fading in and out, she heard a voice: "Don't know why . . . play with such . . . naughty boy."

"Not naughty," protested Brandon.

"You—you are, too," said Charlotte, catching her breath. She thought, Don't act scared or you'll hurt her feelings! "I don't know why she should play with you, either. You could have hurt me with that thing! And I'd just told you not to throw it."

Brandon stuck his lower lip out. "Throw."

"We know that, but there're good ways and bad ways to throw." Charlotte picked up a beanbag, wondering where Susie was. "Don't throw *at* people. Throw *to* people. Gently! Like this." She tossed the beanbag to him. It landed by his feet. She took a deep breath. "Now, throw it to Susie, and she'll try to catch it. Okay?"

Brandon hesitated, looking at a spot near the foot of the crib on the other side, then picked up the beanbag and tossed it, a little harder than necessary. It landed with a chunky beanbag rattle in Susie's invisible hand, and she tossed it to Charlotte, who caught it neatly. "See?" said Charlotte, repressing the creepiness along her spine.

Brandon nodded.

"Now I'll throw it to you, and you try to catch it."

On the one hand, it was a normal game of catch, the beanbag being tossed from one to another, the tosser hesitating and creating confusion as to who the target was, the target standing ready to catch and sometimes failing. But no face gave her signals from the other corner of the crib. No hands urged her to toss. No voice laughed at a catch or a dropped bag. She and Brandon played with empty air.

Brandon talked as often to Susie as to Charlotte, and when he wore out, crawled over to her. Charlotte was too tired to be jealous at that; she was almost too tired to be spooked. Having another baby-sitter on hand, even an invisible one, was a relief.

But what if Bart walked in?

He didn't. And when he called them to lunch, Charlotte knew that Susie didn't go with them to the kitchen because Patchy, on the windowsill, kept right on watching the grackles in the backyard. Brandon told Bart about

Susie coming back, but Bart's only reaction was to ask, as he passed Charlotte the ketchup, "Did you start that up again, or did he?"

"Um—both," said Charlotte. "He behaves better with her in the room!"

Bart laughed, then winced at the sound of the power drill in the garage not ten feet away. "Man, I'll be glad when they're done! It's nearly impossible to do any business on the phone with that going on, not to mention the noise you two made."

"We tried not to be loud," said Charlotte.

"I'm not blaming you. In fact, I'm staggered at how well you do. We all know how hard he is to control when he's been cooped up."

Charlotte, not knowing what to say, ate her hot dog.

Brandon's room was tidy when they returned. All the things he had thrown around had been picked up off the floor and put back in the play box. Susie and Charlotte played dump trucks with him, and telephone, and had a circus with Sock Monkey. Then nothing would do but Brandon and Susie must play airplane. Charlotte lay on the floor watching as he swooped wildly through the air, giggling like a crazy kid and waving to his sister. "Lookit, lookit, lookit me!" A faint drift of sparks burst and faded in his wake almost too quickly to see in the daylight.

"I'm looking," said Charlotte, feeling sick to her stomach. She forced a cheer. "Way to go, Susie!"

"Way go, Susie!" cried Brandon.

At last, it was nap time. For once he was willing to get into the crib, though he demanded indistinctly that Susie sing worms. As Charlotte leaned over the bars rubbing his back, she thought she heard, faint and uncertain, a voice on the other side, singing the song she had heard last night. If she moved her hand through the middle of that sound, it would be like moving her hand through ice water. So she didn't.

Brandon's eyes closed. "Urp goes one," sang the voice, for the third time. "Urp goes two. Urp goes number three."

"That's a weird song for a lullaby," whispered Charlotte, lifting her hand from Brandon's back.

"I know," said Susie. "But Glo liked it."

The voice was little louder than a thought. "How come I can hear you sometimes, and sometimes not?" asked Charlotte.

". . . focus hard," said Susie. ". . . makes me tired."

"Do you—um—do you know why you're here?" There. The big question, and if she got mad, Charlotte couldn't do a thing about it.

A cold, sparkling draft cut through the hot air in front of Charlotte's face, and she wondered how a ghost could breathe. "Promised . . . Gloria . . . stay right here."

"But what—"

Charlotte stopped. The sparkles faded on the air, and she didn't need to feel the hot air where they had been to know that Susie was gone again.

10

The Idea

"You're kidding," said Shannon. "You *played* with her?"

"I don't know if she got it about being dead last night," said Charlotte. "I thought she was mad at me. But she was a big help with Brandon." Currently, Brandon was riding Bart's shoulders, ahead of them on the way to the pool. "And now she's gone again."

"Not for long," Shannon assured her.

"But why does she blink out like that? And if she can go away for a little while, why can't she stay away? I'll tell you one thing for sure, she doesn't want to be here!"

"It's probably like falling asleep," suggested Shannon. "You get tired, and you can't stay awake, but once you're rested, you can't stay in bed. She has to get her energy back."

"I wish she wouldn't. She doesn't belong here!"

"Look on the bright side. At least you've got free baby-sitting help."

Why couldn't Shannon ever get the point? "But this whole haunting thing stinks for her!"

"Oh, it does not. She can fly, right? And she never gets hungry, or has to go to school, and nobody tells her what to do. So what are you feeling sorry for her for?"

Charlotte shrugged.

"If you're going to feel sorry for anybody," said Shannon, swinging her towel, "feel sorry for me! I've got to go to the library for a dumb school project tomorrow."

"I thought you liked the library."

"I like the library for getting ghost books, not for looking up dumb stuff in dumb newspapers on the weekend." She kicked a loose rock in the street, sending it skittering ahead of her. Charlotte thought she felt an idea stir in the back of her head, but Shannon kept talking before she could pin it down. "I'm supposed to go back to the day I was born and the day Dad was born. We've got a list of questions, like what did a pound of hamburger cost and what was on TV and what was the big headline for those days."

"Hey, it might have been something cool," said Charlotte, trying to care. "Want me to come keep you company?"

It would be good to get away from the house.

At least she *could* get away.

Unlike Susie.

Bart paid their way into the pool and looked down at her. "S'matter, Lottie? You feeling okay?"

"I'm fine," said Charlotte. "I was just thinking."

"Well, stop it. You look like you've lost your best friend. Whatever you're thinking about, it isn't important enough to spoil your swimming for."

He was right. She and Shannon played tag and practiced underwater somersaults. The water was cool and bright and wonderful, and the fact that awful things could happen to people retreated to a comfortable distance.

On the way home, she and Shannon held Brandon's hands between them and talked over his head about the trip to the library, and whether it would be better to have someone take them or to go on the bus and be free to check out the downtown mall afterward. "We could buy my mom something," said Shannon. "She's got a birthday next week."

"And we could get ice cream," said Charlotte. "And stop at the arcade. I've got lots of allowance saved."

"That arcade has gang members in it," said Shannon, stopping at the sidewalk in front of her house.

"Oh, it does not," said Charlotte, stopping, too. Brandon, his hands slippery with sweat, wiggled free and ran after Bart. "You always want things to be scarier than they really are. The cops don't let gangs hang out at that mall."

"All they do is make them turn their caps frontways," said Shannon. "You always want to make things nicer than they are. The cops can't keep people out of public places, and you can't wish your ghost away. You're a medium, you know. You'll probably be dealing with ghosts your whole life."

In front of their house, Bart stopped to talk to one of the workmen. The other two workmen reloaded their van, packing up after a day spent putting up Sheetrock. A stack of bricks in the driveway announced their next project—making the raw, new wall that had once been the garage door look like the rest of the house, half brick and half siding, with a window and door.

"I am *not* a medium!"

"You couldn't play games with Susie if you weren't."

"It's got nothing to do with me. I told you, she has to focus. I can barely hear her."

"Look, if it bugs you so much, find out what her unfinished business is with her family and help her go to the light."

"I asked her about that. She said she promised Gloria."

"Promised her what?"

"To stay here. That's not just unfinished business, it's unfinishable!" Again an idea darted across the back of Charlotte's brain. Brandon charged straight past Bart and the workman, holding his arms out and making airplane noises. Charlotte took a step farther along the sidewalk, slowly, to let the idea catch up, but it was gone. "And I better catch Brandon before he gets into anything."

"Oh, you're a slave to that kid," said Shannon. "We don't have to take him to the library, do we?"

"No," said Charlotte. "Mom watches him on Saturdays."

"Brandon!" called Bart. "You come here!"

Brandon turned his head toward Bart, tripped on the edge of the driveway, and went tumbling straight into the pile of bricks.

A shout of dismay rose on all sides. Charlotte, Bart, Shannon, and the workmen all ran forward. The vision of a cut head and blood filled Charlotte's brain so that she barely knew that she saw Brandon snatched back in the instant before his face smashed into the corner of the pile. The trail of sparks faded as Bart grabbed Brandon up from where he had landed, flat on his bottom but unhurt, in the grass by the driveway.

One of the workmen said, "Whew! I thought for sure he'd smashed himself up that time!"

"It's my fault," said Charlotte, the force of her heartbeat shaking her. "I was supposed to be holding him, and he slipped out, and I was talking to Shannon—"

"It's all right," said Bart, holding him up for her to see. "He's fine, though I'm not sure how he wound up falling *backward.*"

"Go oops," said Brandon. "Susie got me."

"You went more than oops," said Bart. "If you'd fallen on those bricks, you'd have split your head wide open. How many times have I told you . . ."

Charlotte looked around the driveway and the yard, as the workmen returned to their business, but no movement of sparks or cool air told her where Susie was.

"See? It's a good thing Susie's around," said Shannon quietly. "Brandon needs as much watching as he can get."

"Yeah," said Charlotte. "But can you imagine babysitting kids like him forever and ever and ever?" Her heart was slowing down. "Thanks, Susie," she whispered to empty air. "I owe you one."

But how did you pay a debt like that?

Charlotte paged through the phone book at the kitchen table while Bart put Brandon safely into his playpen. The first thing she saw under Miller was the notation: "See also Mellor, Millar, Moeller, Mueller, Muller." Ugh! What a lot of names to check! However, there was one Gloria Miller. She picked up the phone, pushed one number, and stopped. What would she say? "Hi, are you the Gloria Miller with the sister who's a ghost?" She laid down the receiver.

Most people didn't stay put, with the same names, their whole lives. Charlotte herself had moved twice since she was five. Mom had changed her name when she married Dad, and again when she'd married Bart. Charlotte could have changed her name, too, but she'd decided not to. But if Gloria and Susie's mom had divorced and remarried, Gloria might have decided to change her name. She'd probably gotten married herself when she grew up and changed her name then. The chance that the Gloria Miller in the phone book was the right one was about zero.

Charlotte put her head down on the table, feeling tired all over and wishing she could shut off for a little while, like Susie. Well, she'd get away from it tomorrow. She and Shannon would do nice boring ordinary newspaper research. . . .

Research.

The idea she'd been about to have all day settled at last, and she knew what her next step should be.

11

The Newspaper

"What if we wanted to find the people that used to live here?" Charlotte asked at dinner. "We could do it, through the real estate agent or something, right?"

"I guess so," said Mom. "Why would we want to?"

"I was just wondering," said Charlotte. "Sparkler Susie's parents could still be alive, couldn't they?"

"Charlotte!" Mom snapped.

"They easily could," said Bart, "and they wouldn't want to hear from us! They moved out because they couldn't stand the sight of this place. I know it's only a story to you, but think about it from their point of view. How would you feel if Brandon—if something happened to him—and fifty years later people called you up and told you some silly story about his ghost?"

"But what if he really *was* a ghost?" asked Charlotte. "What if he was lonesome and scared and wanted to see me again?"

"That's not a relevant question," said Bart, "because there aren't any ghosts."

"You've always been so sensible before this," complained Mom, wiping Brandon's chin. "Why all of a sudden are you so wrapped up in silly supernatural stuff?"

"Ghost," said Brandon. "Fly like Susie."

Hearing Brandon say that made Charlotte's skin prickle. How much of all this did he understand? "Weird things *do* happen. What if there really *are* ghosts? How do you know Susie's not the one playing Tetris on the computer?"

"That's like asking how we know Brandon isn't possessed by a demon when he's particularly naughty," said Bart.

"What if—what if you *saw* something?"

"That's enough!" Mom slammed her hand down on the table. "You're getting morbid! It's that Shannon's fault, isn't it? I'm going to give her folks a piece of my mind about spreading ghost stories!"

"Now, honey," said Bart. "We don't need to fight with the neighbors."

"We don't need scared kids, either! If Shannon and Charlotte can't find anything better to talk about than—than Sparkler Susie, she'll just have to find another friend."

"Kids talk about these things," said Bart. "I did, you did—I bet Sparkler Susie did, if her mom didn't make her stop."

"I *didn't* talk about it," said Mom, "and I'm not talking about it now."

"But—"

"I don't want to hear any more about it!"

Neither do I, Charlotte thought grumpily, but I don't get a choice!

Fortunately, Mom was done being mad by the time Charlotte asked if she could go to the library with Shannon—or maybe it was just that Charlotte didn't know anybody else yet, and the library was a nice safe place to go.

The girls took the bus downtown after lunch on Saturday, while Mom and Bart took Brandon on a string of errands. That left Susie alone in the house, but maybe that was better than being in a house full of people she couldn't talk to.

At the huge multicolored library downtown, the librarian they asked about newspapers sent them upstairs to a section called Texana and Genealogy. Grumbling, Shannon dragged Charlotte into the purple elevator. "This is way too much work," she said. "I don't *care* what hamburgers cost when I was born."

"You care what grade you get, don't you?" asked Charlotte as the elevator carried them upward.

"Why should I? It won't make any difference in a hundred years."

"But you've got to *live* all the time between now and a hundred years." Unless she died, which was likely. But people did live to be a hundred ten. Sometimes. Charlotte tried to picture Shannon dead and couldn't. She tried to picture her old and wrinkled and blowing out a hundred ten birthday candles, and she couldn't quite see that, either.

Shannon went straight to the librarian at the purple desk in Texana and Genealogy and said: "I need to look at old newspapers."

"Sign in, and I'll call you when the machine's ready," said the librarian, handing her a clipboard. "I'll show you where to pull what you need. When you're done, leave them on top of the cabinets."

Charlotte poked purposefully around the bookshelves as the librarian took Shannon around the corner. The books had titles like *New Hampshire Marriage Licences and Intentions, 1709–1961.* When Shannon returned with two boxes of microfilm, Charlotte pointed that one out to her. "If we had a book like that for Texas, we could look for all the Gloria Millers that got married in San Antonio, find out her new name, look for her in the phone book, and tell her about Susie."

"She might not have been in San Antonio when she got married, or it might have been after 1961." Shannon brushed the worn maroon backs of a row of thick books. "You reckon your Millers are in the city directory from back then?"

"We don't know when 'back then' was," said Charlotte. But she pulled out a volume—carefully, because the back was loose and frayed. "These only go back to the fifties."

"Early fifties are after World War II," said Shannon. "I bet we can find my grandparents."

Sure enough, there were the Kohns, at the familiar address. "That means this is too late," said Shannon. "The Millers moved out before Grandma and Grandpa moved in. I wonder—"

"Shannon Kohn," called the librarian.

The librarian showed them how to thread the microfilm, move the picture around on the screen, and focus it. Then she left them alone. Shannon found her birthday and read out the answers to the homework questions while Charlotte wrote them down. Shannon was not impressed with the news of her day until she got to the classifieds. "Ooh, look, there I am!" she said, pointing to an ad, almost too small to read, under Birth Notices.

Charlotte leaned over her shoulder and squinted. "Born to Rachel and Mark Kohn, Shannon Vanessa—I didn't know your middle name was Vanessa."

"That's 'cause I hate it," said Shannon. "How come that kid got a picture, and I didn't?" She pointed to a fuzzy black-and-white photo.

"Because your folks aren't show-offs," said Charlotte. "Look, the death notices and birth notices are together."

"I guess that's so people can find out who their kids are replacing," said Shannon. "Some of these dead people rated pictures, too. I don't think that's fair." She started rewinding the microfilm.

Charlotte felt seasick, but that might have been from watching the microfilm whiz by. "You reckon Susie got a picture?"

"If we knew when she died, we could find out," answered Shannon.

Charlotte's mouth was dry, and she wondered whether she wanted to do this. If she really did, wouldn't she have mentioned it to Shannon before? "We know what day she died. And we know the year was after the war but before your grandparents moved in. I bet we could find her. But we'd—we'd have to hog the machine." She couldn't believe she'd come out with such a lame excuse not to do what she knew needed doing!

"So?" Shannon tugged the rewound reel off of the spindle. "Go pull those years while I'm looking up Dad's birthday. Nobody'll know it's not all part of the same project."

Charlotte's stomach fluttered as she pulled the July boxes for the San Antonio *Light,* 1945 to 1955. It was awful to look up Susie's death as if she were looking up a word in a dictionary—but the notice would give her parents' names. If they were alive—if she could talk to them, without Bart and Mom knowing . . .

It probably still wouldn't do any good.

They finished Shannon's homework, then began working their way through the years. Cranking through all the days they *didn't* want to get at the one they did was a pain. The paper looked funny, and the death notices were even fainter, fuzzier, and harder to read than those in the newer papers.

"You know," said Shannon, after they'd strained their eyes scanning a few, "she might not get a notice, anyway. A lot of people die and get born every day, but there's only a few notices." She cracked her knuckles. "My hand's wearing out."

"I'll do it," said Charlotte. She changed places with Shannon, turned the crank, realized she was going backward, and stopped. "I bet— Oh!"

In the middle of the screen, dark and fuzzy, Susie smiled the frozen smile of someone trapped in front of a school photographer.

12

The Cemetery

GIRL CRITICALLY INJURED IN FIREWORKS INCIDENT

Ten-year-old Susan Miller was taken to the burn center at Brooks Army Medical Center this afternoon for injuries received while playing with fireworks, according to her parents, Robert and Maxine Miller.

"We don't know where it came from," Mr. Miller said. "The only fireworks we bought

> were sparklers and firecrackers." The sole witness, five-year-old Gloria Miller, was too hysterical to question. The children had been playing in the front yard for about half an hour when Mrs. Miller's attention was attracted by a loud report and screams. She found her daughter, with severe burns on her arms, face, and upper torso, in the driveway.
>
> According to the fire marshal, the likely culprit is the cylindrical silver firework known as an M-80. "All fireworks are dangerous, and children should never be allowed to play with them unsupervised; but M-80s and cherry bombs are the most dangerous of the common fireworks, and should be illegal," he said. . . .

"M-80s *are* illegal," said Shannon.

"Probably not back then," said Charlotte, skimming the rest of the article. "The rest is all what the fire marshal says."

"Go to the next day," said Shannon.

Charlotte turned the crank quickly till she reached the next front page, then proceeded more slowly. On the lower half of the very last page before the classified ads was a small article: GIRL INJURED BY FIREWORKS DIES. This story gave the same information about the M-80, added that Susie had died without regaining consciousness at seven o'clock on the evening of July 4, and told people where to send flowers. "Internment will take place July sixth, at 2:00 P.M., in City Cemetery Number Three," Shannon read.

"Internment?" Charlotte asked.

"It means they're going to bury her," said Shannon. She pointed at the address given for the cemetery. "I bet that's the Halloweeny-looking graveyard that the Martin Luther King Day march goes by every year. It's on the right street."

"Do you think, if we went there, we could find Susie's grave?"

"Why would we want to?" asked Shannon. "I thought you just wanted her parents' names."

"It isn't far, is it?"

"Not by bus," said Shannon. "But I'm warning you, it'll creep you out."

"I don't care," said Charlotte, which wasn't quite true.

"There shouldn't be any ghosts in cemeteries," Charlotte declared as they walked to the bus stop. "They're either haunting where they used to live or the place they died, or they're gone to heaven."

"Right," agreed Shannon. "There's nothing in graveyards but bodies—and not even those after a while."

The bright, hot sun beat down on their heads like a hammer. "The worms crawl in and the worms crawl out," Charlotte sang, unsteadily. "They play pinochle on your snout."

"That's the spirit!" said Shannon. "We laugh at death!"

They sang and giggled and sweated while the bus wound its way under the highway, through the Alamodome parking lot, down streets of old-fashioned little houses. They got off at a park, where kids played on the swings, and walked past a Catholic school, as silent and strange-looking as schools always are on weekends. Beyond the school, across the street from a Church's Chicken, they found a cemetery. The wrought-iron gate across the driveway, though locked and barred, did not go all the way to the ground, and the fence was a chain link. "Who do they think they're kidding?" Shannon asked, peering through the bars. "If they want to keep people out, they should try harder."

"Hang on," said Charlotte, reading the peeling metal sign beside the gate. It was a private cemetery, for the members of a local civic group. SAN ANTONIO, HERMANN SONS CEMETERY, PRIVATE PROPERTY. ANYONE CAUGHT VANDALIZING WILL BE ARRESTED AND PROSECUTED BY THE S.A. POLICE DEPARTMENT. "This is the wrong place."

Shannon pointed down the street. "There's another gate. There must be more than one cemetery."

They walked on another block, peering through the chain link at the graves. Most were neatly kept, and many had artificial flowers on them. Charlotte could see why the Hermann Sons Lodge had put up the sign about vandals, though. One grave, for a baby who had been born and died in 1920, had a headless, armless angel on top. What kind of creep, Charlotte wondered, would smash up a baby's gravestone?

The chain-link fence around the graveyard on the next block had vines growing on it, and the iron gate proclaimed it to be St. John's Lutheran Cemetery. Charlotte was just as glad that this wasn't the place, either. Getting over the chain link would have been easy, but what if someone at the Sunglo station across the street saw them and called the police? If all graveyards were closed to keep out vandals, finding Susie's grave would be against the law.

"There's more cemetery on the next block," said Shannon, pointing. "Geez, can you believe this? There's graves as far as the eye can see here!"

They walked up the next block. This time no gate faced New Braunfels Avenue, but a driveway led in from the side street. The cable that should have closed the drive lay in the dirt. The graves looked bare and helpless here, with fewer trees to shield them from the sun. The sign was so faded they had to stand next to it to read it: CITY CEMETERY in black letters on a white background, then, barely legible: # 3.

"This is it," said Shannon.

"Yeah, but where do we look for Susie?" asked Charlotte, waving her arm at the muddle of family plots and individual graves, huddled wherever there was room, the drive picking its way through them.

"Hey, this was *your* idea," said Shannon. "Now we've come, we might as well do our best." She reached into her pocket for change. "Let's get a drink at the Sunglo, and then get to work."

So they wandered the graveyard, drinking a cold, biting mixture of Sprite and lemonade, reading the names of dead strangers off the newer stones of polished gray granite. The older, less legible, stones were white and often mossy, broken, eroded, or crooked, as if the earth had shifted restlessly. German and Spanish and Anglo names, the 1890s and the 1970s—all were mixed together. Shannon started taking notes about the different tombstones—white ones with lambs for babies, open books for married couples, flat slabs and fancy pillars, stone tree trunks, even a wooden cross with a broken arm.

Charlotte felt worse and worse. Did anybody remember any of these people? How many were like Susie, lost and lonesome in the spirit world? Why did their families let their stones break and their plots overgrow with weed? With an uneasy jerk of her heart, Charlotte realized that she had no idea where her own great-grandparents were buried, or what their names had been, or what they had looked like. And someday her own great-granddaughter would not know about her. Would not want to think about her, because she was dead, and the fact of death was too terrible to think about.

She lifted her head to see more graveyards stretching beyond this one, on the next block, and the next, and the next. So many dead people! And this was just the tip of the iceberg. This cemetery went back to the late nineteenth century, but there had been people in San Antonio way before that: Anglos and Mexicans and Spanish and Indians—where were *they*?

Charlotte left Shannon scribbling next to the wooden cross, and walked toward a cedar tree, bigger and older than cedars usually got, so that it looked less like a bush and more like a real tree. She leaned against the shaggy, warm-smelling bark and sipped her drink. Nearby a mockingbird sang, its notes as sweet and piercing as the drink. Mockingbirds didn't live as long as humans. Someone had once told her that no two mockers had the same song.

Could a mockingbird have a ghost?

Charlotte stared, unfocused, at the nearest grave. Someone had planted purple-leaved, pink-spotted coleus in flower urns flanking the gray double slab. A married couple, but with only the man's half filled in. Charlotte wondered how it felt to be the one left alive, to come here and see that blank space, waiting for your name. Robert Miller's wife—

Robert Miller.

Charlotte had seen "Miller" three times already, and once a Susan Miller, dead at the wrong age on the wrong day. This would be another wrong Miller family. She walked to the neighboring grave, a smaller, older stone at the shade's edge. The name Miller ran across the top, but English ivy spilled out of the urns over the rest. Charlotte lifted it aside.

"Miller. Susan Jean. Greater love hath no man."

The day of death was the Fourth of July.

13

The Note

Charlotte stared at the stone, numb, until she heard Shannon call to her.

"Hey, Charlotte! Look at this!"

Charlotte looked up and waved at her to come over. "No! I found her!"

Shannon, clutching her notebook, her book bag bobbing behind her, picked her way among the graves, trying not to walk on anybody. She dropped to her knees next to the stone. " 'Greater love hath no man.' I wonder what they meant by that?"

"How would I know?" asked Charlotte. "It's from the Bible somewhere. The point is, she's here, and her father's there."

"Okay, you've found her." Shannon hiked her shoulders. "Does that mean you want to go home now?"

"Not yet," said Charlotte. "You notice anything different about these graves?"

Shannon looked from one to the other. "The potted plants are a cool idea, but I think marigolds would be nicer."

"Coleus and ivy don't need any taking care of, hardly," said Charlotte, remembering a couple of recent conversations Mom and Bart had held about landscaping, what to plant, and who would take care of the yard. "But somebody trims it sometimes, or the ivy'd be all over Susie's grave, and it's not. And I bet it's almost time to do it again, because it's pretty long."

"Okay, I see that," said Shannon. "Who do you reckon it is? Mrs. Miller, or Gloria?"

"I bet Susie'd be just as happy to see either one," said Charlotte. "So I'm going to write a note."

"Are you crazy? Neither one's going to believe you've got Susie's ghost!"

"I don't care. Give me a sheet from your notebook."

Now that contacting the Millers was a real act instead of an idea, Shannon's enthusiasm seemed to have evaporated, but she flipped to a clean sheet and tore it out. "It won't do any good," she said. "The paper'll blow away, or it'll get rained on and dirty and she won't be able to read it, or—"

"I don't *care,*" said Charlotte. "Anyway, since when does it rain in summer?" She leaned the paper against the flat, smooth surface of Mrs. Miller's side of the tombstone, and wrote, twisting her face in concentration as she tried to word it properly.

Dear Mrs. Miller or Gloria,

My name is Charlotte Verstuyft and I live in your old house, the one you sold off fifty years ago. I think you should know that Susie is still there. Only little kids and animals can see her unless she concentrates real hard. My little brother, Brandon, and my cat, Patchy, both see her all the time, and I have seen and talked to her some. Sometimes she goes to sleep, or something, but she can't go anywhere because of promising Gloria to stay put. She'll be awake on the Fourth of July for sure because that's her anniversary and ghosts have to be around then. She is terribly lonesome and wants to see you real bad. I think maybe y'all are the only ones who can help her go on to the light. Please call soon. Before the Fourth of July if you can, because otherwise I won't know when to tell you she'll be around.

Love,
Charlotte Verstuyft

Charlotte frowned at this, feeling that there ought to be more, but uncertain what that more ought to be. She wrote her phone number underneath her name and folded the paper tightly.

"Where are you going to put it so it won't blow away?" asked Shannon.

"In the ivy," said Charlotte as she tucked the note into the leaves. Shannon found a suitably heavy rock in the unpaved drive and weighted it down. Satisfied, Charlotte stood up and dusted off her knees. "That's the best I can do," she declared. "What was it you wanted to show me?"

They poked around the graveyard a little longer, then caught a bus back into town, visited the mall, bought Shannon's mother a pair of earrings, and returned to the library. If they didn't come back with some books, everybody'd ask what had taken them so long. Shannon wasn't sure how her folks would react, but Charlotte had no doubts about hers. "They'd say it was morbid and unhealthy and all your fault so we couldn't do things together anymore," she said, "and if I know what they're going to say, I don't know why I should have to hear them say it."

The days between the trip to the graveyard and the Fourth of July were much like the days before, only hotter. The office gradually began to look like an office instead of a garage. Mom had decided against giving the

Kohns a piece of her mind, at least not until after the big block party. "Charlotte'll meet more of the neighborhood kids at the party, and they can dilute the effect of Shannon without our having to fight with our neighbors," she told Bart at a time when she thought Charlotte was in the bathroom out of earshot.

Bart promised they could go to Fort Sam Houston for the fireworks in the evening, and Brandon got all excited, though Charlotte wasn't sure he understood what fireworks were. She couldn't muster up any enthusiasm for them this year, and she really wished she could shut him up in front of Susie. Every day he wanted to know if it was fireworks day yet.

Every time the phone rang, Charlotte jumped and her heart stumbled. What if Gloria called when Susie wasn't around? How could she get them together if she didn't know where Susie would be? And what would happen if Mom or Bart answered the phone? At night, she lay awake, planning the conversation in her head. Sometimes, as she reworded her explanations, Patchy would stiffen beside her and a shower of sparks would drift through her room.

The Fourth of July began with a bang as someone lit a string of firecrackers in the street at seven o'clock. The day was windless, hot, and smelled of gunpowder. Charlotte rolled out of bed, wondering if she was alone.

"Susie?" she called softly. "You going to be okay today?"

A cold touch on her hand, gone almost before she noticed it, answered her. "Remember, nothing awful can happen to you anymore," she said. "And we'll all take care of Brandon so nothing happens to him. And I'll be extra careful, so nothing happens to me. Okay?" Again, the chill touch came and went. "They have this block party every year," she said. "And nobody's ever been hurt." Shannon would have mentioned it, if anyone had.

In the next room, Brandon set up a shout that verged on being a song: "Yankee Doodle wenna town, riding on a stony, stuck a noodle inis hat and call it macaroni!"

"Oh, geez, I hope he doesn't do that all day!" Charlotte sighed, then thought she heard Susie laugh, next to her ear.

It was too hot to eat much, so everybody had melon and yogurt for breakfast. Mom dressed Brandon in a brand-new white jumper with red and blue stars, and she took him into the backyard, secure in the knowledge that the workmen had packed away all their stuff and shut up the office tight. Bart French-braided Charlotte's hair so it would be off her neck, and she spent almost half an hour picking out the right dress and necklace to go with such a sophisticated hairdo.

Shannon came banging on the door while Bart was working on their contribution to the picnic. "The guy who was supposed to connect the sound flaked out," she said, charging in. "Mom said Bart could do it since he used to be a pro."

"I haven't worked sound for five years, and I'm elbow deep in potato salad," Bart protested.

"It'll come back to you, your hands will wash, and Charlotte and I can make potato salad," said Shannon relentlessly. "The baton twirlers are lining up already, and they can't do their routine without the Sousa marches."

So Bart called through the open window to Mom, washed his hands, and left to rescue the baton twirlers. Behind the big bowl of steaming potatoes he had lined up all the ingredients neatly on the counter: mayonnaise, mustard, vinegar, pickles, olives, celery, onions, chopped eggs, and paprika. Charlotte worked her way down the line, dumping in ingredients while Shannon stirred till bits of potato flew onto the Formica. She tasted, "More mustard. Yuck, what do you want to put olives in for?"

"They're the best part."

"Gross! They make me puke."

"So pick them out of your helping." The phone rang, and Charlotte dumped in the olives before picking it up. "Happy Fourth of July."

Someone was crying—not hard and loud, like Brandon; not softly and endlessly, like Susie; but in a sniffing, halting way, as if her crying muscles were worn out. "Charlotte?" the voice gasped, in between the tears. "Charlotte Verstuyft?"

"Y-yes, ma'am?" said Charlotte.

"This is Gloria. Gloria Miller Thiel."

"Gloria?" Charlotte's planned conversations deserted her.

Shannon stopped stirring and nearly knocked Charlotte over, rushing to put her ear next to the phone.

"I don't know how you knew my name, young lady," gasped a voice. "And I don't know what possessed you to come looking for my sister's grave, but of all the heartless, mean things that've ever been done to me—"

"But I didn't!" blurted Charlotte, with an abrupt, hideous sense of how nasty her note would have seemed if she had been Gloria and hadn't believed in ghosts. "I'm sorry! Oh, please don't cry! I didn't mean to make you feel bad, honest! I wouldn't have done it if it wasn't all true! Susie's here, and she cries at night, and baby-sits my brother, and sings worms to him, but she's lonesome. She can't get off the property, and she's waiting for you to come back—"

"How did you *know*?" demanded Gloria. "About the promise? I never told anybody. Not even my husband! How did you find out?"

Suddenly, violently, all of Charlotte's hair stood up

with cold. Shannon stepped back with a gasp. Soft but clear in the sunlit kitchen, Susie's voice sang:

"Now everybody loves me, nobody hates me,
Better urp up them worms—"

Charlotte dropped the receiver, but it did not fall. Susie continued to sing. Smaller and more distant even than the ghost voice, Gloria croaked: "Susie? Susie, is that—?"

"Gloria?" said Susie. "I stayed right here. Where are you?"

"I'm coming," sobbed the voice. "I'll be— I'll be— Wait for me!"

Then there was a dial tone. The receiver drifted into the cradle.

14

Gloria

Susie hovered underneath the kitchen ceiling, her head buzzing. Shannon and Charlotte jabbered below her, but their voices made no sense. She did not focus on her hearing. She did not focus on her sight. She was barely Susie anymore; she was an idea. Gloria . . . coming back. Her little sister, Gloria, was coming back.

Her mental picture of Gloria, faded and worn over time, was suddenly clear again. Gloria, her hair brown and curly, her baby fat clinging roundly to her face and arms. Gloria, in print dresses and jumpers, with her baby doll and her red ball, endlessly playing fetch with Moxie.

The voice on the phone hadn't sounded like Gloria.

People never sounded like themselves on the phone.

Charlotte had said something about Gloria, something important, but though Susie strained to think clearly, the image of her little sister, coming home, swallowed up everything else.

Outside, someone heated charcoal. Pulses of Sousa music blared and died, blared and died. Shannon returned to the potato salad, pounding in more mustard with movements even jerkier than before, while Charlotte ran into the backyard and talked to her mother over Brandon's head. Sylvia brought him in, traded him for the finished potato salad, and carried it out front, where the neighbors were setting up long tables on the sidewalks. Brandon fussed restlessly in Shannon's grasp. Charlotte ran to get the playpen, while Brandon yelled, "Susie!" His shrill young voice pierced the fog that surrounded her. "Flying!"

Shannon stared. Susie wondered what she saw as she extracted Brandon from Shannon's arms and flew him gently to the end of the room and back. "You're getting too heavy for this," she told him. "Pretty soon you'll be too big to carry." She set him down in his chair. Patchy strolled in on her way to the food bowls and stopped to hiss at her as usual. But it didn't matter. Not with Gloria coming back!

"Susie play!" Brandon scrambled down from his chair and charged off for the living room—open and un-air-conditioned, for once, the computer blank and dead. Susie followed, and Charlotte dragged the playpen outside through the front door. "What's the magic word?" Charlotte asked.

"Susie play *please!*"

Susie played with him, Sock Monkey, and a dump truck until Charlotte returned, looking slightly to the left of Susie. "We're putting Brandon in the playpen in the front yard," she said, loudly and slowly. "Susie, will you stay with him till Gloria gets here? We want to be able to find you." Without waiting for an answer, she picked him up and carried him out.

"What are you, crazy?" Susie trailed after them. "Putting him out there with all those fireworks and grills and things? He can get out of the playpen, you know!"

No, she didn't. He had only figured it out in the last day or two, and Susie'd always managed to coax him back in before anyone came back into the room. There was such a thing as being too good a baby-sitter.

No cars were allowed to drive on the cul-de-sac today, and everyone kept their pets inside. Sprinklers turned in yards, not to water the grass, but for kids in shorts or swimsuits to run in and out of. Barbecues and tables covered with salads, buns, and paper plates already lined the sidewalks as neighbors wandered across one anothers' yards, set up flags, paused to talk. In Shannon's yard, her father poured ice-cream mix into a series of machines that were plugged into outlets in his garage. At the end of the block, the baton twirlers practiced while Bart and Shannon's mom fiddled with the sound system. Susie didn't bother with her ears. She never did on the Fourth of July. She didn't like the explosions and shouting. She played with Brandon, a little absently, keeping a look out for kids with fireworks. Shannon and Charlotte stood by the playpen, shoulder to shoulder, talking, with more movements of their hands and heads than usual. Arguing? Excited? Nervous? What did *they* have to be nervous about?

"Susie fly!" said Brandon.

"Not outside," said Susie. "Flying's private. Gloria's coming, Brandon! I'm going to see my sister, Gloria!"

A plump woman in blue jeans and a sleeveless blouse trotted up the street and stopped in front of the blue house. Susie thought: "I know her," but she didn't remember from when. Her curly brown hair was streaked and speckled with gray, her face red and blotchy, as if from heat or tears. She walked up to Charlotte and Shannon, holding out her hand.

Her voice, clear and strong, pierced Susie's unfocused ears and set up shivering echoes all through her. "I'm Gloria," she said. "I heard . . . I heard . . . Is it real? Is Susie here?"

The buzzing in Susie's head grew louder as Charlotte

answered. Gloria? That wasn't Gloria! Without realizing she had done it, she shot up out of the playpen. Brandon cried out in protest, and she hovered, looking down on them all, as she had looked down on so many, many people. The important thing that Charlotte had said hovered out of reach of her brain. Brandon waved Sock Monkey at her, and the woman walked toward him. She looked up, following the direction of his eyes till she looked straight at Susie, and pushed her hair back from her face. The face . . . the face . . .

It was an unbearable face, like those of her mother and father and Gloria, not belonging to any of them.

"It seems so . . . so impossible," said the woman's inescapable voice. "That she could have been here, all this time."

Charlotte and Shannon stood on either side of her, gesturing. Brandon threw Sock Monkey straight at Susie; she let it zip through her.

"Is she . . . is she here, now?" asked the woman.

Charlotte nodded vigorously, her mouth moving. It occurred to Susie to focus on her hearing, but she missed whatever Charlotte said. The Sousa music, clear but not too loud, played in the background.

"No, there doesn't," said the woman, her voice wobbly. "Everything makes sense now. I w-wasn't dreaming, and it's all m-my fault—"

Susie's heart twinged.

"No, it's not," said Charlotte. "How could it be?"

"You were only five when she died," said Shannon. "It's not *possible* for anything to have been your fault."

"Oh, yes it is." The woman fished a crumpled handkerchief out of her pocket and blew her nose. "I killed her."

"An M-80 killed her," said Charlotte, and the image flashed across Susie's mind. An M-80, a silver cylinder with a sputtering fuse, gleaming in the sun.

"*My* M-80," said the woman. Music danced cheerily through the air as she sniffed and blew and got control of her voice. "We'd gone into the front yard to play. We were supposed to play with Moxie—with our little dog—but the fireworks scared him. She decided to put him in the garage, and she told me to stay put while she did it. But I didn't. A boy came by—I don't remember him, really. He was just a boy. And he lit a silver firework, a big one, and tossed it on the driveway and rode off. And I w-wanted, I wanted that pretty firework so bad—"

"Oh," gasped Charlotte. "Oh, you didn't!"

A bright silver firework with a sputtering, short fuse, gripped in two chubby hands that would not throw it away.

"I did," said the woman. "I went to the driveway, and I picked up the firework, and I—I carried it toward the garage to show to Susie."

Susie had all her focus in her ears, but she felt the pain in her hands and face, and she saw the terrible image as if it were in front of her, not drifting vague ages away. The bright blue day—the open garage door—Gloria, coming toward her, with silver death in her hands. She did not remember moving, but she remembered grabbing, fighting, shoving Gloria, and then the bang, and the horrible, horrible pain that had sent her soaring into the sky.

"I have no idea what I was thinking. I actually shouted at her, told her it was mine. And she shoved me, wrenched it out of my hand, and she—she lost her balance and fell right on it, clinging to it like— She had it in her hands when it went off." Gloria took a shuddering breath. "If I'd let go when she told me to—if I hadn't brought it for her to look at—if—"

"You were *five!*" protested Charlotte.

"I was five and I killed my big sister," said Gloria.

"You did *not!*" cried Susie, but she couldn't even hear herself, though Brandon started crying in sympathy.

"It was an—an accident," stuttered Shannon, hugging herself against the horror. "It was that boy's fault. I'd like to kick his rear end for him!"

"It was an accident that should have happened to *me,* not to *her,*" said Gloria.

"No!" Charlotte declared, bending over Brandon in the playpen. "*She* was the big sister. It was *her* job to take care of you! Getting blown up herself was *lots* better than watching you get blown up!"

Susie could have hugged her.

"There is no 'better' for this. And you haven't heard the end of it." She sounded more steady now. "She came back. After Mama and Daddy made me understand that Susie wasn't coming back, ever—she came back. She rubbed my back and sang worms, and promised . . . promised to stay right here. Forever. And the day we moved. She tried to come with us, but she couldn't get into the car."

"Because she'd promised to stay right here?" asked Shannon in a small voice.

"I think so," said Gloria.

"She's been waiting for you to come back," said Charlotte, picking Brandon up and rocking him. "You and your mom and dad. It's okay, Brandon."

"Well. I'm here now," said Gloria. "And I can't see her. I wonder if she even still wants to see me, after fifty years."

"She's hard to see," said Shannon. "But we know she's around. She picked Brandon up earlier."

"But I want you to see me, Glo!" cried Susie, trying to focus on her body, feeling it sink. She choked.

"Susie cry," said Brandon.

"Where is Susie, Brandon?" asked Charlotte.

"Right there," he said, pointing, his voice squeaky with concern. "Don't cry, Susie! Don't cry!"

"I'm trying not to," said Susie, gasping, but she had no lungs to hold air.

"Oh, my goodness," said Gloria, squinting. "Those sparks falling—"

"That's her," said Charlotte.

Dimly, Susie was aware of the woman walking toward her, holding out her hands. "Susie," she said. "Susie?"

Susie swooped down, focusing, and took her hands.

15

Home

Charlotte saw Gloria shiver, beginning at the tips of her fingers, and knew that Susie had touched her. "I'm so sorry," whispered Gloria, to the sparkling, shimmering swirl of air in front of her. "I never meant for any of this to happen."

"Susie cry!" said Brandon. "Mean lady!"

Charlotte squeezed him. "You hush," she said, "or I'll take you inside. That's Susie's sister. They had a fight and now they're making up." She didn't know how much of that he grasped, but he shut up. Already his weight dragged at her arms, but she didn't want to put him down. Anything might happen if she did that. She did not think about what she meant by "anything," or wonder what she thought could happen to him with fireworks and traffic both forbidden. She just supported him securely with her arm under his behind and didn't protest when he pulled the top of her dress uncomfortably sideways. Shannon kept her eyes fixed on Gloria, hugging herself as if she were cold, though the day was so hot it was hard to breathe.

Gloria's hand gripped sparkling air, hair standing up on her arms, her face damp with sweat. "Susie," she said. "I'm sorry I made you stay here. I didn't know what I was asking you to do. And I'm so sorry I deserted you. I tried to tell them. But this house was so unbearable when we couldn't see you in it! If they'd known you were here we never would have moved. Never." She peered into the sparks, as if searching for Susie's face. "You don't have to stay anymore. There's a place for you. Daddy's already there, and Mama and I will get there someday, too. But please—could I see you once more before you go? Just one more time, so I'll know you're not mad at me?"

Sparks clustered, red, white, and blue, hovering into a striped pattern, settling into a human shape—bare arms and bare legs, sandals trailing above the grass, a brown ponytail.

"Mad at you?" said Susie, distant but clear. "I'm so

glad you're alive! You grew up! And you came back!"

Gloria hugged her, shuddering with cold as her skin overlapped with Susie's.

Susie floated back from the hug—did she know how cold she made people?—a puzzled frown flickering across her happy face. "You're older than Mama."

"Yes," said Gloria. "I'm a grandma, actually. My younger girl has a baby. I have two daughters. Suzanne, who's an architect and doesn't want to have children, and Diane, with the baby. His name is Daniel. Mama's living in an apartment for people who don't get around well by themselves. And Daddy— Susie, are you listening?" She put out her hand, and Susie took it, her fingers protectively on the outside. Dismay distorted her smile, and the edges of her sundress turned to sparks.

"Everybody grew up but me."

"I know," said Gloria unsteadily. "I wish I could fix it. But I can't. All I can do is set you free."

"You came back. You can stay."

"It's too late for that. This isn't your house anymore."

"Then where do I live now?"

The question could barely compete with the recorded sousaphones down the block. Susie shimmered like the air above a barbecue.

"You don't live anywhere anymore," said Gloria gently, trying feebly to let go, but Susie squeezed her hands.

"Then how do I go home?"

She's confused again, thought Charlotte, as Gloria tried again to hug the cold air. Or maybe she doesn't really want to know. Brandon wiggled, slipping in her sweaty arms. She put him back into the playpen, touching her finger to her lips to shush him. He looked from her to Susie, frowning.

Charlotte watched as Susie's arms and legs faded. She would be gone in a second, but not gone for good. Not if they couldn't convince her.

Charlotte stepped up and put her hands into the cold where Susie's hands fluttered, nearly invisible.

"Think, Susie," she said. "I know it's hard, but you can. Keep remembering that you're dead."

". . . don't want . . . remember." Susie's face was transparent as a reflection in water, but her voice solidified, like a radio station tuning in from the static around it. "I don't want to be dead."

"Forgetting won't make you any aliver," Charlotte pointed out. "Do you want to spend the next fifty years waiting for kids that can see you, so you can baby-sit? Trying to focus hard enough long enough so I can hear half of what you say? Because that's all that's left. This is as good as it gets."

Charlotte saw the idea sink in, though Susie's face was so faint it made her eyes water to find her. "I don't know how to be dead," said Susie.

"You didn't know how to be born, either. But it worked out."

Her hands were numb. Susie withdrew, shimmering toward Gloria, who reached out, then drew back. "I don't know, either," she said. "But you've already been doing it for fifty years. And Daddy—Daddy's been doing it for seven years. I'm sure he's looking for you."

Susie's face wasn't focused enough for Charlotte to tell whether she understood now that her father was dead. "Then why didn't he come here?"

"I don't know. Maybe he can't. Maybe he didn't think to, or maybe by the time he thought of it he'd gone too far to come back. But I'm sure he's looking. And Mama's looking forward to seeing you again—when she, when she—Susie, honey, she's *old.* It's been fifty years!"

Susie focused, momentarily, face and shoulders and helplessly upturned hands, looking down at Brandon, who held up his arms and called, coaxingly: "Susie play?"

She drifted toward him and hovered over the playpen, but she didn't reach down.

"He's getting bigger all the time," said Charlotte. "He can almost hold a conversation. How big are they when they stop seeing you? What if . . . what if he forgets you when he can't see you anymore?"

Brandon stood in the playpen, reaching for her. Susie hovered, just beyond his grasp, and looked over at Gloria.

"They grow up so fast," said Gloria. "I grew up so fast.

And here you are. Oh, Susie, I'm so sorry you didn't get to grow up! I don't know if going on will give you that. But staying here won't give you anything."

"I'd have to forget," said Susie, her voice surprisingly clear. "If I stayed. I can't stand it when I remember. But I'd have to forget you came back. And I can't stand that, either."

Brandon climbed out of the playpen, as easily as if he'd done it a dozen times, and jumped to grab Susie. She swooped down, hugged him, and looked at them all over his shoulder. "It doesn't work," she said, bleakly. Then, in a firmer voice. "It doesn't work."

"Susie fly?" asked Brandon hopefully.

Susie shook her head, her ponytail thinning out into a slow-dropping trail of sparks. "No, Brandon. I have to—I have to go now. You mind Lottie, now. You be good."

Brandon's face compressed unhappily. "Dawanna."

Charlotte took him by the shoulders and looked Susie in the eye. For the first time she could see that they were brown eyes. "I'm sorry," Susie said to Brandon, and kissed him on the forehead. "Bye-bye."

"Bye-bye?" Brandon waved doubtfully.

Charlotte wrapped her arms around him as Susie swooped through her. "Good-bye," she said—or Charlotte thought she said—on her way to Gloria, where she dissolved into sparks and hesitated—looking around. How would she know which direction to go? Charlotte was beginning to fear that they had made her face facts for nothing when the sparks began to move again, swirling around Gloria three times before beginning to rise, slowly at first, then faster and faster, until at last they soared across the sky, and vanished.

"Hey!" protested Brandon. "Where Susie go?"

"Home," said Charlotte, holding him still as he tried to follow. "And she's not coming back, so you'd better get used to minding me without her!"

Brandon stuck his unsteady lower lip out. "Don't wanna."

"Tough," said Shannon, staring at the place where the sparks had dissolved into blue sky. "Susie has other things to do besides baby-sitting you."

I hope she does, thought Charlotte, wanting to cry; but if she did, Brandon would begin to howl. Instead she wiped his face and said, "S' okay. *I'm* still here," waiting for him to start bawling.

But he didn't; instead he clung damply to Charlotte as she rubbed his back. Gloria, still shivering, gazed at the empty sky. The relentless happiness of the marches and the neighbors and the children in the sprinklers seemed rude and out of place. No one had noticed anything, not even Mr. Kohn in the next driveway. No one knew that the street had changed forever, one of its traditions fled.

"You'll warm up in a minute," Charlotte told Gloria,

when the silence among them became too much to bear.

"I'm sorry I yelled at you," said Gloria.

"S' okay," muttered Charlotte, embarrassed. "I guess I didn't think how it would sound to you when I wrote the note."

"What . . . what made you think of looking for the grave?"

"I got curious, I guess," said Charlotte. That didn't sound like enough. She looked down at her baby brother, still staring unhappily at the sky. "Susie was a big help with Brandon. I wanted to do something to help her out."

"And I thank you for it," said Gloria. "And for helping me. I've lived my whole life feeling so awful. Everybody told me it wasn't my fault. I never believed that till today. It feels so . . . amazing . . . to believe it. Not good, but . . . to know she forgave me—" Gloria stopped, as if her voice had gotten unfocused like Susie's, and she had to take a couple of deep breaths before she went on. "For years we wouldn't talk about her, and then, when my father died, and I found out he and Mama had reserved the spaces next to hers—it was like a door opening in my head. Her grave looked so small and sad and alone, and that cemetery is such a mess—I knew it wouldn't help her or Daddy to take care of the graves, but I couldn't think what else to do for them."

"So you went back every Fourth of July?" asked Shannon. "Didn't that make you feel worse, reminding yourself?"

"Fourth of July was never my favorite holiday, anyway," said Gloria. "At least this way I spend it doing something, not hiding in my room with the blinds down and wincing every time a firecracker goes off. Suzanne and Di thought I was the most unfair mother in the world, not letting them have fireworks."

"Fireworks," said Brandon, jerking his eyes off the sky to look at Charlotte accusingly. "Today. Daddy said!"

"That's right," Charlotte assured him, swallowing the nasty feeling that Brandon now expected her to take away everything he wanted. "We'll see fireworks tonight. Speaking of Daddy, he's coming this way. Um—"

"I won't tell him," said Gloria.

"But what—" began Shannon.

Charlotte stepped on her foot, and she yelped as Gloria met Bart at the sidewalk. "I'm Gloria Miller Thiel," she said. "I used to live in your house."

"What'd you do that for?" demanded Shannon quietly.

"That poor lady has enough to put up with, without you bugging her."

"I don't want to bug her," protested Shannon. "I need to ask her some more questions, that's all. Like how exactly did the promise go, and could her dog see Susie, and—"

"That would bug her," said Charlotte.

"Those are important questions!"

"Only to you," answered Charlotte, letting go of Brandon and watching him as he toddled across the grass to Bart. "You need to pay attention to how other people feel."

"Okay, smarty. If I'd paid attention to how you felt about it, there never would have been any séance, and you never would have known that Susie didn't know she was dead, and you never would have tried to talk to her, and—"

"Okay, okay. But quit while you're ahead."

"You're welcome to stay," Bart was saying to Gloria. "In fact, come next door. I bet our neighbor'd be thrilled to meet you. You girls hang on and look after Brandon another minute, okay? Brandon, stay with Charlotte. I'll be right back."

"Fireworks!"

"Later." Bart took Gloria next door.

"I wonder where Susie went exactly," said Shannon.

"Heaven, I guess," said Charlotte, wondering what it was like, if they had hot summer days and band music and the smell of hot charcoal. Briefly she remembered all those graves, and how one day her body would be in one, while her real self was . . . where?

Bart came back, gesturing to turn her and Shannon loose upon the transformed block. They walked down the sidewalk, away from the huge questions of the past few weeks, toward a holiday that seemed more real with every step. Red, white, and blue hung from the edges of tables, and every house sprouted a flagpole. Mr. Kohn's ice-cream freezers danced on a layer of condensation on the driveway. People drank lemonade from sweating plastic cups, turned kabobs and hot dogs on grills, and sang along with the canned band. Charlotte found herself marching to the beat, in lockstep with Shannon, and the familiar tune formed words in her mind. They looked at each other, waiting for the right place in the sound, beginning to grin in spite of themselves, and at the proper moment roared in unison: "Be kind to your web-footed friends!"

Freed by the sousaphones, they ran singing toward the baton twirlers, setting aside the need to wonder or to remember, setting aside everything except enjoying being right here, right now.

Susie dove up into the hot blue sky. How Brandon would love this part, when his turn came! A hawk dodged her lazily, but there were no thunderheads today. She remembered the thunderhead from the first time. She remembered the relief of that first soaring, the freedom from pain, the lightness, until she weighted herself down.

But not today. Today Gloria was safe, and Daddy was waiting..

What if she couldn't find him?

What if, in the end, there wasn't anyplace to go?

What if, what if, what if . . .

The sky darkened to midnight and stars exploded across her vision like fireworks. She remembered the Gonzalez baby now, all the babies and children and pets and the long loneliness of her haunting. She remembered the first time ever that Gloria came home, a little bundle of wailing blankets. How Susie had hated her then! But that feeling was meaningless now.

She remembered the time before Gloria, when she had her parents to herself, remembered a time before speech, a time before fear, when the world was darkness and the rhythm of Mama's heart. She remembered her terrified first plunge into light.

She rose and she remembered, remembered and rose, until she had gone too far for fear to snatch her back.